SEVEN YEARS

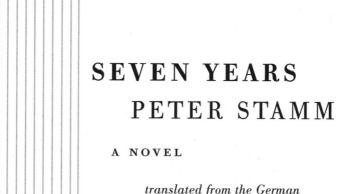

SEVEN YEARS
PETER STAMM

A NOVEL

translated from the German
by Michael Hofmann

OTHER PRESS *New York*

Originally published in German as *Sieben Jahre* by S. Fischer Verlag GmbH, Frankfurt am Main, 2009.

Translation copyright © 2010 Michael Hofmann

Production Editor: *Yvonne E. Cárdenas*
Book design: *Simon M. Sullivan*
This book was set in 11.5 pt Bodoni Light by Alpha Design & Composition of Pittsfield, NH.

10 9 8 7 6 5 4 3 2

Library of Congress Cataloging-in-Publication Data

Stamm, Peter, 1963-
   [Sieben Jahre. English]
   Seven years / Peter Stamm ; translated [from the German] by Michael Hofmann.
       p. cm.
   ISBN 978-1-59051-394-1 (trade pbk.) — ISBN 978-1-59051-395-8 (ebk.)   1. Married people — Fiction.   2. Husband and wife — Fiction.   3. Triangles (Interpersonal relations) — Fiction.
4. Psychological fiction.   I. Hofmann, Michael, 1957 Aug. 25-
II. Title.
   PT2681.T3234S5413 2011
   833'.914—dc22
                                                          2010040658

Light and shadow reveal form.

LE CORBUSIER

SEVEN YEARS

S onia stood in the middle of the brightly lit space; she liked to be at the center of things. Her head was slightly lowered, and she kept her arms close to her sides. She was smiling with her lips, but her eyes were narrowed, as though she were dazzled or in pain. Like the paintings on the walls, to which no one paid any attention but that were supposed to be the occasion for the presence of all these people, she seemed somehow not there, or only superficially there.

I was smoking a cigarillo, and watched through the plate glass gallery window as a good-looking man went up to Sonia and spoke to her. It was as though she woke up from her slumbers. She broke into a smile and touched glasses with him. His lips moved, and I could see an almost child-like astonishment come over her, then she smiled again, but even from where I was I could see she wasn't listening to the man, she was thinking about something else.

Then Sophie was standing next to me. She seemed to have something on her mind as well. She said, Mama is the most beautiful woman in the world. Yes, I said, and I stroked her hair. She is, your mama is the most beautiful woman in the world.

It had been snowing since morning, but the snow melted as soon as it touched the ground. I'm cold, said Sophie, and she slipped back into the gallery, through the door that someone had just opened. A tall bald man had come out, with a cigarette between his lips. He stood far too close to me—as though we knew each other—and lit it. Ghastly pictures, he said. When I didn't reply, he turned and took a couple of steps away. Suddenly he seemed a little uncertain and awkward.

I kept watching through the gallery window. Sophie had run in to Sonia, whose face brightened. The good-looking man, who was still next to her, looked sternly, almost offended, at the girl. Sonia bent down to Sophie, and the two of them had a short conversation, and Sophie pointed outside. Sonia shielded her eyes with her hand and peered in my direction with a strained smile, creasing her brow. I was pretty sure she couldn't make me out in the darkness. She said something to Sophie and gave her a little push toward the door. I felt a momentary impulse to run away, to merge with the crowds getting off work and striding through the light that poured out of the gallery. The passersby glanced cursorily at the elegant, nicely dressed people within, and then hurried on their way, heading home with the rest of the crowd.

I hadn't seen Antje for almost twenty years, and even so I recognized her right away. She must be about sixty, but her face was still youthful. Well, she said, and kissed me on both cheeks. Before I could say anything a young man with a silly-looking ornamental beard appeared by her side, whispered into her ear, and pulled her away from me. I saw him lead her to a man in a dark suit whose face was familiar, maybe from the newspapers. Sophie had collared the man who a moment ago had approached Sonia, and was flirting with him, to his evident embarrassment. Sonia listened with an amused expression, but once more I had the feeling her thoughts were elsewhere. I went over to her and laid my arm around her waist. I enjoyed the man's jealous look. He was asking Sophie how old she was. Guess, she said. He pretended to think. Twelve? She's ten, said Sonia, and Sophie said, you're mean. You're very much like your mother, said the man. Sophie thanked him with a curtsey. She's the most beautiful woman in the world, she said. She seemed to know just exactly what was going on.

Do you mind if I take Sophie home now? Sonia asked. Antje will probably have to stay till the end. I offered to take Sophie home myself so she could stay, but she shook her head and said she was really tired. She and Antje had the whole weekend to look forward to anyway.

Sophie had asked her beau to fetch her a glass of orange juice. He asked if he could get anyone else a drink. Will you stop ordering other people around? I said. I wonder who she gets it from, Sonia said. She bit her lip and looked down at the ground and then into my eyes, but I pretended I hadn't heard. We're out of here, she said, and kissed me quickly on the mouth. Try not to make any noise when you get home.

The gallery started to empty, but it was a long time until the last of the visitors had gone. In the end, there was only Antje and me, and an elderly gentleman whom she didn't introduce. The two of them were standing side by side in front of one of the pictures, talking together in such quiet voices that I instinctively left them alone. I flipped through the price list and kept glancing at the two of them. Finally Antje put her arms around the man, kissed him on the forehead, and walked him to the door. That was Georg, she said, I used to be crazy about him. She laughed. Weird, isn't it? That was a hundred years ago. She went to the bar and came back with two glasses of red wine. She held one out to me, but I shook my head. I've given it up. She smiled doubtfully, emptied her glass in a single swallow, and said, well in that case, I'm all set.

The gallery owner had left the keys with Antje. She spent ages flicking the light switches until it was completely dark. Once outside, she slipped her arm through mine and asked if the car was parked nearby. It was still just snowing. What weather, she said. Next time we should meet in Marseilles. She asked me if I liked the paintings. You've gotten a little calmer, I said. Subtler, I hope, said Antje. I don't understand art, I said, but unlike before, I could imagine having a painting of yours up on the wall at home. Antje said she wasn't sure if that was a compliment or not.

I asked her if she had invited Sonia's parents to the opening. I had expected them to be there. Antje didn't reply. If you want to visit them, I can loan you the car, it's just a hop and a skip to Starnberg anyway. Antje still didn't say a word. Not until we got to the car did she answer that she hardly had any time, and she was too tired to go driving around the countryside. Getting the show ready had really taken it out of her. I asked her if there was anything the matter. She hesitated. No, she said, or maybe there is. They've gotten old and narrow-minded. Surely they always were, I replied. Antje shook her head. Of course Sonia's parents were conservative, she said, but her father at least

5

used to be genuinely interested in art. She had had many conversations with him about it. Of late, he had become more and more inaccessible, perhaps it was an age thing. He didn't have any use for anything new, and had turned bitter. He doesn't need to agree with me, she said, but I wish he would at least listen to what I have to say. The last time we met, we had a huge argument about Gursky. Since then I haven't felt like seeing him.

I wondered whether there might not be other reasons for Antje not to see Sonia's father. I often suspected there might have been something between them. When I ran it by Sonia once, she reacted indignantly, and said her parents had a good marriage. Just like us, I thought, and said nothing more.

Even though there wasn't much in the way of traffic, it still took us a long while to get clear of the city. Antje didn't speak. I looked across to her and saw she had closed her eyes. I thought she was asleep when she suddenly said she sometimes wondered if she had done me a favor back then. How do you mean? What with? Sonia wasn't sure, Antje said. For a while neither of us spoke, and then Antje said Sonia wasn't sure whether we were a good match. You mean if I was good enough for her?, I asked. You had potential, Antje said, I think that was her word. The other boy . . . Rüdiger, I said. Yes, Rüdiger was fun to be with, but he wasn't focused enough. And then there was someone else. She tried to recall the name. The one who later married the musician. Ferdy?, I said. Maybe, said Antje.

6

I couldn't imagine Sonia ever being interested in Ferdy.
It didn't last long, Antje said. Did she really have a thing
with him? We were stuck at a light, and I turned to Antje.
She smiled apologetically. I don't think she slept with him,
if that's what you mean. Didn't she tell you?

Sonia never did talk much. It often felt as though she'd
had no previous life, or whatever it was had left no traces
except in the photograph albums on her bookshelf, which
she never took out. When I looked at the pictures, I had
the sense that they came from another life. Now and then I
asked Sonia about her time with Rüdiger, and she gave me
monosyllabic replies. She said she never asked me what I'd
done before either. It doesn't bother me, I said. After all,
you're mine now. But Sonia was stubbornly silent. Sometimes I wondered if it wasn't that there was just nothing to
say.

Antje's smile had changed, she looked a little mocking
now. You men like to make conquests, she said. Try and see
it in a positive light. She checked through her possibilities,
and chose you.

A car honked behind me, and I accelerated so fast the
tires squealed. And what was your part in the whole thing?,
I asked. Can you remember the first night the two of you
stayed at my place?, asked Antje. Sonia went to bed early,
and we sat up and looked at my pictures together. I had half
a mind to seduce you. I liked you, clean-cut little college
kid. But instead I just led you up the garden path, and told

you Sonia was in love with you. And the next day I gave her a spiel. What did you do that for? Antje shrugged her shoulders. Are you annoyed? Her question sounded serious. It was for fun, she said finally, I put in a good word for you. There was something with another woman, a foreigner, if I remember. Ivona, I said, and I sighed. That's a long story.

I'd been sitting for hours with Ferdy and Rüdiger in a beer garden near the English Garden. It was a hot July afternoon, and the sunlight was a dazzling white. We'd handed in our final thesis projects ten days before, and in another week we had to go and defend them. We didn't have much else to do except while away the time and give each other courage. All three of us had chosen the design of a modern museum on a site bordering the Hofgarten, and we were sketching out our plans and pushing notepads back and forth. Our voices were loud and excited, and we didn't care that the other customers kept turning around to look at us. Rüdiger said my plans reminded him of Aldo Rossi. I was offended, and said what did he know? There are worse people to imitate than the old masters, said Ferdy, but Alex tries to reinvent the wheel every time he draws something. Then tell me where Rossi fits in, I said, and pushed my plan across the table. But Rüdiger had already moved on. He was talking about Deconstructivism, saying the architect was the psychotherapist of pure form, and more bullshit of that type.

A couple of girls were sitting at our table. They were wearing light summer dresses and were attractive enough in an uninteresting way. After a while we got talking. One of them worked for an advertising agency, and the other was studying art history or ethnology or something like that. It was a flip sort of conversation, made up of one-liners, jokes and comebacks, all going nowhere. When the girls paid to leave, Ferdy suggested we all go to the English Garden together. They hesitated briefly, and conferred in whispers, then the advertising girl said they had other plans, but we might meet up later at Monopteros. As they left, they had their heads together, and after a couple of steps, they turned and waved and laughed at us.

I'm having the blonde, said Ferdy. The brunette is much prettier, said Rüdiger. But the blonde is really stacked, said Ferdy. There you go, deconstructing again, said Rüdiger. Two women between three guys doesn't work. Ferdy looked at me. You'd better find yourself a girl. Why me?, I protested. Ferdy grinned. You're the best-looking of the three of us. That girl over there has hardly taken her eyes off of us.

I saw a woman reading a couple of tables away in the shadow of a big linden tree. She was probably our age, but she was completely unattractive. Her face was puffy, and she wore her midlength hair loose. Presumably she had gotten a perm some time ago, but it had grown out, and her hair was hanging in her face. Her clothing looked cheap and worn. She had on a brown corduroy skirt, a patterned blouse in wishy-washy pastel colors, and a scarf around her neck. Her nose was reddened, and a few crumpled-up tissues were on the table in front of her. While I was still taking her in, she looked up and our glances met. Her face twisted into an anxious smile, and in a sort of reflex I smiled back. She lowered her eyes, but even her shyness seemed inappropriate and disagreeably flirtatious.

Women are helpless in the face of his charms, said Ferdy. He'll never get her, said Rüdiger. You wanna bet? Before I could answer, he went on. I bet you don't get her. There was something sad about his eyes now. I said I wouldn't even take her if she was offered. Well, we'll just have to see about that, said Ferdy, getting to his feet. The woman was watching us again. When she saw Ferdy making straight for her, her expression changed to a mixture of dread and expectation. He's mad, I groaned, and turned away. The whole thing was embarrassing to me already. I looked around for the waitress. Surely you won't bail at this stage, said Rüdiger, come on, be a man. What's the sense of this, I said, and stretched my legs. My good mood was gone, I felt useless and rotten, and was angry at myself. It was as though the voices and laughter faded into the background, and through the sound I heard the approach of steps across the gravel.

Meet Ivona, said Ferdy. She's from Poland. This is Rüdiger, and *this*—is Alexander. He was standing behind me, I had to look almost vertically up at him. Have a seat, said Ferdy. The woman put her glass down on the table, and next to it her tissues and her book, which was a romance novel with a brightly colored cover showing a man and a woman on horseback. She sat down between me and Rüdiger. She sat there with her hands folded in her lap and a very straight back. She looked restlessly between us. There was something stiff about her posture, but her whole appearance was somehow sagging and feeble. She seemed to have given up all hope of ever pleasing anyone, even herself.

Isn't the weather lovely, said Rüdiger, and giggled foolishly. Yes, said Ivona. But it's hot, said Ferdy. Ivona nodded. I asked her if she had a cold. She said she had hay fever. She was allergic to all kinds of pollen. All kinds of Poles?, asked Ferdy, and Rüdiger laughed like a drain. No, grass, dust, said Ivona, not batting an eyelid. And so it went on. Ferdy and Rüdiger asked her stupid questions, and she answered them seemingly unaware that she was being made fun of. On the contrary, she seemed to enjoy their interest

in her, and smiled after each one of her monosyllabic replies. She came from Posen. I thought you were from Poland, said Rüdiger. Posen is a town in Poland, Ivona replied
patiently. Her German was almost accentless, but she spoke
slowly and cautiously, as if not quite sure of herself. She
said she worked in a bookstore. She was trying to improve
her German, and supporting her parents back home. Her
father was an invalid and her mother's earnings weren't
enough for them both.

From the very outset, Ivona was disagreeable to me. I
felt sorry for her, and at the same time I was irritated by
her docile and long-suffering manner. Instead of holding
Ferdy and Rüdiger back, I was closer to joining in their
mean games. Ivona gave the impression of a natural-born
victim. When Ferdy said we had arranged to meet up with
two girls in the English Garden, and didn't Ivona want to
join us, I felt like protesting, but what would have been
the use? Ivona hesitated. Four o'clock at Monopteros, said
Ferdy, turning to us. Shall we go?

We were there in good time. The two girls arrived shortly
after us, only there was no sign of Ivona. She's not coming, I said, thank God. Who's not coming?, asked one of
the girls. Alex's girlfriend, said Ferdy, and he turned to me
and said, you can wait here for her, you know where we're
going.

Rüdiger said quietly he'd keep me company. We sat down on the steps of the little temple, and he passed me a cigarette. The ugly ones are the hardest to pull, he said. Because they never get a man, they think they're something special. I shook my head. Nonsense. Ivona reminded him of a girl he'd gone out with in the early years of high school, Rüdiger said. Subsequently, he'd not been able to tell himself why. In fact he'd already been in love with Sonia at the time, but she'd been too much for him, with her looks and everything. I must have gone for the other girl because of fear, said Rüdiger, or else I was trying to get a rise out of Sonia. Brigitte wasn't a looker, and she was really hard work, and most of the time she was in a bad mood. I wasn't allowed to do more than kiss her and grope a little bit. But somehow I wasn't able to break up with her. She manipulated me, I never quite understood how. He went on talking, but I stopped listening. My own mood hadn't improved. I was tired from the beer, and sweaty, and I felt unwell. I asked myself what I was doing waiting for Ivona if her company was so unpleasant to me. Perhaps some remnant of manners, perhaps curiosity, or perhaps just because heading off would have needed a decision on my part, and my lack of initiative was crippling me.

Ivona arrived twenty minutes late. She was wearing the same outfit as at lunchtime, plus a little beige cardigan, even though it was still warm. She didn't apologize and didn't say what had made her late. All right then, said Rü-diger, and he stood up.

We met the others at a place by the lake where we often went. The girls said hi to Ivona, but more or less ignored her after that. We had brought blankets, and Ferdy had a couple of lukewarm bottles of beer. We lay there torpidly, passing bottles around, and talking about all kinds of things. Ivona didn't drink anything, and she didn't contribute to the conversation. She just sometimes blew her nose and smiled a stupid-looking smile. Once or twice she made as if to speak, but one of the others got in first, and she gave up. I noticed that she was watching me. Each time I looked across to her, she looked away, as though I'd caught her in the act. Again I felt like hurting her, being rude to her. Her ugliness and pokiness were a provocation to me, her desire to belong exposed us and made us laughable. I wondered how I might shake her off. Shall we go cool down?, I finally asked. We grabbed our things. Ivona hadn't said anything, but she trotted along behind us to the Eisbach. The greater part of the meadow was already in shadow, and the few people who were still there clustered in the last patches of sunshine. I had expected the presence of nudity to deter Ivona, but she showed no reaction, and silently sat down on one of the blankets, as though she was entitled to it. Ferdy said he was going for more beer, and took off.

The girls were wearing bikinis under their dresses, and Rüdiger and I stripped and ran naked down to the water and jumped in. When we returned a little later, the girls were lying side by side, talking together softly. The blonde had her top off, and turned onto her stomach as we approached. Ivona was sitting in the shade, she hadn't even taken her cardigan off. She looked at me in surprise, and my nakedness embarrassed me, and I pulled on shorts and pants. Then I played Frisbee with Rüdiger. The girls seemed to have no interest in us, presumably they were talking about what they were going to do that night and we didn't figure in their plans. And that's what happened, Ferdy returned finally, and they said they had to go. Ferdy half-heartedly tried to keep them, but I think basically we were all relieved when they went. Only Ivona made no move to leave.

By now the whole meadow was in shadow. The last of the bathers had dressed and gone, and were probably drifting through the bars and beer gardens of the city. I was seized by a mixture of melancholy and expectation, it felt as though the present moment had shrunk to something infinitesimally small, separate both from the past and from whatever lay ahead, which felt distant and notional. Rüdiger and Ferdy started talking architecture again, but it wasn't like before. Ivona sat off to one side, her arms clasping her pale legs. She didn't say anything, but she was still getting in the way. Ferdy, who was sitting with his back to her, made choking motions with his hands, and leaned forward to me and whispered, I think we have to throw her in the water or else we'll never get rid of her. Rüdiger heard Ferdy and said half aloud, you asked her, she's on your watch. She's Alex's responsibility, said Ferdy. I didn't know if Ivona could hear what we were saying, but she didn't react anyway. She had rested her head on her arms and was looking into the trees. It's no use, said Rüdiger, and stood up.

We cleared our stuff. Ivona got to her feet awkwardly and watched as we rolled up the blankets. When we left, she followed us, without our having asked her to. She was always a couple of feet behind. At the count of three, let's run, said Ferdy, and he sprinted off, but after a few steps he stopped and waited for us to catch up to him.

We went back to the beer garden where we'd been for lunch. We had to sit at a table with strangers. Ivona sat next to me. Again, she didn't say a word, she didn't even seem to be listening to our conversation. Later on, a couple of friends of ours came by, and we had to squeeze together. Ivona was pressed against me, and I felt the softness and warmth of her hips and thighs.

Eventually, my head was reeling with alcohol and noise, I dropped my hand on Ivona's thigh and absentmindedly started stroking her. I wasn't caressing her exactly, it was more like an animal lying next to another animal for shared warmth. When I got up shortly after and waved good night, she got up too, and followed me like a dog following its master. As we left the beer garden, she said she had to go to the ladies' room for a moment. I thought about making a break for it, but by now I was turned on by the idea of being with her. It wasn't the usual back-and-forth, the game of trying to seduce a woman. I had the feeling Ivona was giving herself to me, and I had absolute power over her, and could do whatever I liked with her. I felt utterly indifferent to her. I had nothing to lose and nothing to be afraid of.

It was a long time before Ivona emerged from the restroom. I asked if I should walk her home. She said it wasn't far. We went through a small park. The air felt cooler, and there was a smell of wet earth and dogshit. At the darkest point, I grabbed hold of Ivona and kissed her. She let me, and she didn't resist when I groped her breasts and bottom. When I tried to undo her belt, she turned away and took my hand.

She lived in a student residence hall for women. She walked up the stairs ahead of me. I was feeling a little more sober than before, and it slowly dawned on me what an idiotic thing I was doing, but I was too excited, and it didn't seem possible to turn back now. Ivona unlocked her room and switched on the light. No sooner had she closed the door behind us than I embraced her again, and dragged her over to the narrow single bed. I tried to undress her, but she wouldn't let me. She twisted and struggled with surprising agility. I kissed her and touched her all over, and pushed my hand down the front of her skirt, but her belt was so tight, I could hardly move my fingers. My hand was pressed flat against Ivona's belly, and I could feel her woolly pubic hair. Ivona was whimpering, I couldn't tell if it was desire or fear or both. I hadn't been so excited in ages, maybe because I so completely didn't care what Ivona thought about me. I tried to undo her belt with my free hand. Again she struggled. I said some stupid nonsense or other. She murmured no, and please no. Her voice sounded dark and soft.

When I woke up, I was muzzy and hardly knew where I was. It was brightening outside, the room was in twilight. My head hurt, and I needed to pee. I was shirtless, Ivona had all her clothes on, only the top buttons on her blouse were undone.

While I pissed into the sink, I opened the mirror cabinet, which was stuffed with shampoo samples and unfamiliar medicines. I turned and saw that Ivona was awake and watching me. I said, I'm going now. Then she got up and came over to me and whispered into my ear, I love you. It didn't sound like a declaration of love, more like the statement of an immutable fact. I reached for my shirt and T-shirt. Ivona watched me dress with something like entitlement, her eyes were full of pride. I walked out without another word.

I stopped outside the dormitory to get my bearings. I couldn't remember which way we'd gone the night before. The birds in the trees were fantastically loud, and for a moment I had the ridiculous idea that they might attack me. I asked myself what I was doing here, and how things had ever gotten so far. The whole business was embarrassing to me, and I hoped no one had seen me leave with Ivona. At the same time, though, I felt strangely exhilarated. Everything I'd previously experienced with women struck me as a sort of game in comparison to the night I'd just been through. I had felt grown up with Ivona, and responsible, and perfectly free.

I lived in one of the bungalows in the Olympic Village. It was a tiny place, but my friends in shared apartments or student dorms were all jealous of me. There were hundreds of these bungalows along narrow lanes surrounded by towering apartment buildings, and they really were like a sort of village. They had been built for competitors at the Olympics. After the games, the area was handed over to students. I paid three hundred marks a month for a little house that was roughly 250 square feet. Downstairs there was a walk-in closet, a kitchenette, and the legendary "Nice" shower, a plastic bath unit where you felt you were in a spacecraft. Upstairs was the bedroom and study. One wall of the study was glass, and there was a little veranda outside. To save space, a bunk bed was installed at the top of the stairs. The village was full of stories of couples falling out in the course of wild nights, but presumably that was just student talk.

The bungalows had been run up quickly and weren't in good condition. The windows were poorly insulated, and even so you had to air out the space all the time, because otherwise you got mold in the walls. The student union had provided us with paint for the facades. Some people had made proper works of art, others had scrawled political slogans on the walls. Some of the paintings looked like children's drawings.

There were always parties in the village, and spontaneous barbecues. It was noisy, especially in summer, which made it hard to concentrate on your work. You could hear everything from the bungalows on either side. I had a German lit student next to me. I barely knew his name, but I knew all about his sex life, and I heard every quarrel and every reconciliation with his girlfriend. Sonia, who was taking the same courses as me, sometimes came to visit. She was interested in the architecture of the village, and later on she would come and study with me. One hot summer afternoon, when we were both cramming architecture history, we could hear shouting from next door. I was about to knock on the door to complain when it got quiet. Shortly after that, there were the loud shrieks of pleasure of a woman. Sonia didn't understand at first, and said shouldn't we check up on what was happening. I don't think they need help, I said laughing. Only then did the shoe drop. I said I should have studied German, where you didn't have to work so much, and had time for other things. Sonia blushed, and said she was going to the bathroom. When she returned, the noise still hadn't stopped, and after a few more minutes, she said she had to leave, she had a date. From then on we did all our cramming in the library.

It was before seven a.m. when I got home. Everything was peaceful in the village, and the paths were deserted. I put on the coffee machine and took a shower, then I set off for nowhere in particular. I felt euphoric and needed exercise. I headed for the city center and thought about the future. Everything seemed possible, nothing was going to get in my way. I would find a position in a big architecture firm, in time I would set up on my own, and realize big projects all over the world. I walked through the city, staring at the windows of car dealerships, and already pictured myself at the wheel of some luxury model, going on tours of inspection from building site to site.

I went to the library and read a long newspaper article about a wave of refugees from East Germany, and somehow that went with my feeling of freedom and adventure. Everything seemed possible, even if the commentator urged caution and doubted the imminent collapse of the GDR. At noon I had a sandwich, then I moved on. I bummed around the city, bought myself a pair of pants and a couple of white T-shirts. When I returned to the student village in the evening, I was tired and satisfied, as if at the end of a long day at work.

I went to bed early, and even so I didn't wake up until noon the following day. It was the telephone that woke me. It was Sonia. She asked me if I was doing anything. No, I said, just recovering from the strains and stresses of the final project. We agreed to meet for lunch near the library.

My relationship with Sonia wasn't altogether straight-forward. She had caught my eye on the very first day of school, but I had only got to meet her through Rüdiger. We got along well, and sometime we started doing our drafting together. She was more gifted than me, and had more ap-plication. But she was generous-spirited, and would never have trashed someone else's work, the way Ferdy and I did. She wasn't uncritical, but she was always fair, and whatever her critique might be, it always seemed to be positive. She was just as popular with the professors as with the students. She was able to admire people, and maybe that's why she was admired herself by others. She and Rüdiger seemed to be a dream couple. They could have been married, the way they planned parties and asked us to their parents' homes, as though they had already come into their own. At one of those parties, I met Alice, and we had been going out for several months now. Then Sonia and I broke up with our partners at about the same time, in the middle of exam pressures—maybe that brought us closer to one another. My breakup with Alice was rough, and Sonia, who was a friend of Alice's, had spent nights hearing all about what a son of a bitch I was, and how badly I had treated her. Remarkably, none of that seemed to affect us in any way. Quite the contrary, it was at that time that we grew really close. First I thought it was Sonia's intention to bring Alice and me back together, until one day she said Alice mustn't hear about us meeting, because it would wreck their friendship. Rüdiger knowing didn't matter, they had ended it amicably and with no bad feelings. When you saw the two of them, you might have been forgiven for thinking they were still an item. I asked Sonia what had caused their split. Oh, she said, and made a vaguely deprecating gesture.

Sometimes I entertained the idea of falling in love with Sonia myself, but however plausible it was as an idea, it didn't seem at all appropriate. Perhaps we knew each other too well, and our friendship was too cemented. One time I tried to hint at something. Wouldn't it be perfect, I said, if Alice started going out with Rüdiger, and the two of us . . . What an idea!, said Sonia laughing. And she was right. I couldn't picture her as my girlfriend, not in bed, not even naked. She was certainly very beautiful, but there was something unapproachable about her. She was like one of those dolls whose clothes are sewn onto their bodies. Although, Sonia said, Rüdiger and Alice would make a good couple. So would we, though. It would finish Alice, said Sonia. Anyway, I don't have time for a relationship at the moment. She first had to concentrate on getting a job. She wanted to go abroad, and a serious relationship would just get in the way. I'd like to see you head over heels in love, I said, so badly that it hurts! She laughed. Trust me to say something like that.

I got to the café before Sonia, and watched through the window as she crossed the street toward me. She was wearing white pants and a white sleeveless T-shirt, and she was tanned. When she walked into the café, the whole place turned to stare. She came up to my table and brushed a kiss on my cheek. As she sat down, she looked briefly around, as though searching for someone. The waiter was at hand before I could even call him.

Sonia talked about a competition she wanted to enter, a day care for a big industrial company. She put on her glasses, which I liked her even better in, and showed me her sketches. I made a couple of suggestions, which she turned down. I'd had better ideas before, she said. I told her I hadn't been sleeping well. She looked at me with mock sympathy, and went on talking about her project and integration and shelter and the personality of the children and their uniqueness and potential. My client is the child, she said, and pushed her glasses up over her hair, and laughed.

Sonia was the absolute opposite of Ivona. She was lovely and smart and talkative and charming and sure of herself. I always found her presence somewhat intimidating, and I had the feeling of having to try to be better than I actually was. With Ivona, the time went by incredibly slowly, full of painful silences. She gave monosyllabic replies to my questions, and it was a constant struggle to prolong the conversation. Sonia on the other hand was the perfect socialite. She came from a well-off background, and I couldn't imagine her doing or saying something unconsidered. She was bound to have a successful career. She would find a niche in the design of social housing, and get a seat on various boards, and bring up two or three children on the side, who would be clean and just as well-behaved and presentable as she was. But Sonia would never say to a man that she loved him, the way that Ivona had said it to me, as if there was no other possibility. Ivona's declaration had been embarrassing, just like the idea of being seen in public with her, but even so the thought of her love had something ennobling about it. It was as though Ivona was the only person who took me seriously and to whom I really meant something. She was the only woman who saw me as something other than a good-looking kid or a rising young architect. Ever since waking up, I kept thinking of her, and I was sure I would have to see her again, if only to free myself from her. She had told me she worked in a Christian bookstore. It couldn't be all that hard to find her.

Sonia was talking about a torchlight parade that she had gone on, for the victims of the Tiananmen massacre. The night I had spent with Ivona she and a few like-minded people had marched from Goetheplatz to Marienplatz, and had marked the Chinese sign for sorrow in lighted candles on the square. According to Buddhist beliefs, the souls of the deceased would go looking for a new body at the end of forty-nine days, she said. It was so moving, I cried. She seemed to be surprised by her own emotional outburst. I only hope your soul doesn't find a new body for itself, I said, that would be a shame. Sonia looked at me as if I'd personally shot down the Chinese students. I've got to go, I said. She asked me if I planned on going to Rüdiger's farewell party. I couldn't say yet.

I found three Christian bookstores listed in the phone book. I went to the first of them, but they said they didn't give out information about people who worked there. I took a look around the place. When I didn't see Ivona anywhere, I went to the next place. The manager here wasn't so cagey. He said he didn't have any Polish girls working for him, and there wouldn't be any at the Claudius bookstore, the third one on my list, either, because that was Protestant. He thought about it for a moment. The parish church of St. Joseph in Schwabing had a small shop attached to it, where they sold books and knickknacks. Maybe my girlfriend worked there. She's not my girlfriend, I said.

I had to go once around the church before I saw the store. It was in an adjacent building, in a small recess. A couple of steps led up to the door next to a display window with a few candles and a couple of yellowed-looking pamphlets. *Jesus and TV*, *I Lift Up Mine Eyes to Thee*, *The Everlasting Bond*, things like that.

I looked through the glass door but saw no one. When I walked in, I set off a little bell. It took a moment, and then the velvet curtain parted at the far end. The back room was in bright sunlight, and for an instant Ivona looked like an apparition, bathed in light. Then the curtain fell shut behind her, and the room was once again in dimness.

Ivona looked at me attentively, and without a trace of recognition. She sat down on a chair behind the counter and busied herself by straightening some stacks of miniature saints' pictures. I looked at the books, which were arranged by theme on a couple of shelves: Mission, Help through Faith, Marriage and Family, Sects and Other Religions. There was even a category called Witty and Provocative. I pulled down a book of clerical jokes. On the cover there was a drawing of a lion kneeling down before a priest, paws folded in prayer. I put it back and turned to Ivona. She still wasn't noticing me. I went over to the counter and stared at her until she raised her eyes. My image of her had changed in memory, and seeing her in front of me now, I wondered how I could possibly have wanted her so much yesterday. Her expression was anxious, almost submissive, and I felt disgusted by her again. Without a word I left the shop. After a few feet, I turned and looked back. Ivona was

standing pressed against the glass door, she looked satisfied,
or perhaps just apathetic, as though she really didn't care
whether I stayed or left, as though she knew for sure that I
would be back.

I went home and took out my thesis again. In three days'
time I would have to defend it, and I had the feeling I
had forgotten everything I had pondered over the last few
months. I leafed through the drawings and sketches. Rüdiger was right, my design was derivative, it lacked originality
and force. While I'd been working on it I'd been conscious
of a vague energy, a creativity, but I hadn't known in which
direction to take it. And then, without my really knowing it,
I'd followed my idol. It wasn't even Rossi's buildings that
impressed me so much as his polemics against modernism,
his melancholy which maybe wasn't anything more than
cowardice. Sonia had often poked fun at my old-fashioned
taste. She said Rossi's buildings looked as if he'd taken out
his children's building blocks and played with them.

My work looked shallow and unimaginative to me. Even
so, I felt pretty sure I would pass. But it bothered me just
being mediocre, and to have to admit to myself that I wasn't
the genius I always dreamed of being. Feeling rather disgusted with myself, I put away the papers. I thought of Ivona
and tried to sketch her face from memory, but it was more
than I could do. I called Sonia, but there was no answer.

I ate a snack, and then took myself for a walk. I avoided those places I normally went to with Rüdiger and Ferdy, I didn't feel like running into them in case they asked me some uncomfortable questions. I walked through the city, feeling very much alone. I was shocked to realize that there was only one person I wanted to see, and that was Ivona.

It took me a while to find the student residence. The doorbells only had numbers next to them, no names, and I had no idea what Ivona's number was. I stood in front of the residence, smoking. Finally a young woman came out, and I managed to wedge my foot discreetly in the door before it snapped shut. I stood there while she unlocked her bicycle and rode away.

The buildings must have been from the fifties, the floors were tiled gray, the white on the walls had yellowed, and the banisters' plastic insulation had been worn away in places, showing the metal below. Even though I'd been pretty drunk on the occasion of my first visit, I found Ivona's room without much trouble. On the door was a little number plate, like in a hotel. Below that, Ivona had put her own name, with a difficult surname written out in a childish hand, which I forgot right away and don't know how to spell to this day. I knocked, and Ivona let me in. She didn't say anything, but she stepped aside and let me in, as though she'd been waiting for me. The TV was on, some historical costume drama with romantic music. I shut the door behind me and went up to Ivona, who shrank back, with a sort of cunning expression on her face. When she reached the window she couldn't go any farther, and I seized her hands and kissed her palms and her soft whitish arms. Ivona squirmed a little, then she seemed to give in, and dragged me away from the window. She moved to the bed and fell back into it without taking her eyes off me. Her expression was vacant, like an animal's. I lay down on top of her and went on kissing and embracing her and felt through her thin top for her breasts. She let it happen, only when I tried to undress her she resisted, just as determinedly as the first time. In the background, the music swelled to some sort of crescendo, the film was reaching its high point, or perhaps it was just over. I was very turned on, but it wasn't the standard feeling of being with a girl, not a physical excitement, but excitement of feeling, a warm, dark sensation, a kind of overwhelming safety. I felt no shame as I pulled off my clothes, even though I guessed how ridiculous we must look, a naked man rubbing himself against a woman in ugly old-fashioned clothes. I couldn't care less. Ivona was breathing deeply in and out, her hands were clasped across my back, as though to hold me to her. Without anything happening, I had the feeling she was giving herself to me.

This time I didn't stay overnight, though again when I left it felt like a sort of flight. Ivona had said nothing most

of the time, she didn't say she loved me, only from time
to time emitted a little gasping sound I was familiar with.
When I took her hands and tried to lead them to me, she
pulled away. When I finally gave up, tired and unsatisfied
and still aroused, and we were lying together side by side in
the half-darkness, I naked, she with creased, loose clothes,
I asked, what are we doing here? What's happening? Then
she said she'd prayed that I would come to her. Her voice
was the voice of a little girl who was completely convinced
her prayer could change the world. I don't believe in God,
I said. That doesn't make any difference, Ivona said. I
laughed. Do you really think God's got nothing better to do
than attend to your love life? She didn't respond, but when
I looked at her, she again had that proud and rather simple
expression on her face that she had had that afternoon at
the door of the bookstore. I was mad with her, I could see
myself tearing the clothes off her body, holding her by the
hair, and taking her against her will. Her expression didn't
change. It was the self-complacency of the saints in the
little pictures in the shop, which seemed to be saying any
wrong you do me will only tie you to me even more tightly.

I sat up and rubbed my eyes, full of shame at what I was
thinking. When Ivona touched my back, I jumped. She said
she had prayed that I would talk to her. She had sat close
to me a couple of times in the beer garden, but I hadn't noticed her. I shuddered. The notion of being Ivona's chosen
one had something eerie about it. Why me? She gave no

reply. I have to go, I said, and quickly got dressed. I tied my laces on the stairs.

For the next few days I avoided Ivona. I should have been preparing my defense, but instead I started again from scratch. I got up early in the morning and made a new set of sketches. At first they weren't up to much, but in spite of my continual failure, I got the feeling my thoughts were getting sharper, I was starting to understand something that was more important than form or style or structural engineering, and against all reason I felt optimistic, and was enjoying my work. It was as though I had the answer in my brain, and just needed to lay it bare, clear away all the debris of my training and find the single gesture, the single line that was true to me.

My original blueprint had been elaborated from the geometry of the floor plan, I had worked it up from the space afforded by the size of the plot and the permitted height of a building, the way a sculptor might conceive a figure from a block of stone. The result was a purist construction, not without some appeal as a model, but completely unoriginal and unthought-out as to its interior. This time I tried to work from the inside, from the exhibition space, not the front elevation. I pictured myself as a visitor to the museum, and developed the structure of the building in an imaginary tour of the rooms. I was proceeding not from construction so much as from intuition, trying on the different rooms like clothes. Often I would stand in my study with eyes shut, pushing the walls this way and that, checking the angle and the quantity of the light, groping my way forward. If someone had seen me, they would surely have thought I was crazy. But over time what evolved was a system of rooms, corridors, and entrances that was more like a living creature than a building. Only after that did I turn to the shell of the structure, which really was pretty much just that: a shell.

It was very hot in the bungalow, and I spent whole days in my underwear behind closed blinds. I drank great quantities of coffee till I broke out in cold sweats, and didn't eat till I felt almost sick with hunger. In the evenings I would go out to get a couple of bottles of beer and to pick up a kebab, which I had wrapped and took home with me. In the student village there was loads going on just as the term was ending, every night there was loud music and the sound of festive parties from nearby bungalows and the central plaza. I kept out of everything, sat on my little terrace, looked at the sky, and thought of Ivona. I pictured her in front of me, standing in the communal kitchen of the student lodgings, making herself a simple dinner, scrambled eggs maybe, or boiled potatoes, and taking them to her room and eating alone at her little desk. When she was finished, she went back to the kitchen and cleaned up, maybe she exchanged a few words with another Polish girl she knew to talk to.

But before long she said she was tired, and she went back to her room and sponged herself down with a washcloth. That was the most erotic vision I had of her, standing at her sink and washing her belly with brisk movements, her shoulders, her soft pendulous breasts. Even though the room was hot, the cool washcloth gave her goose bumps. She pulled on a thin oversize T-shirt that showed the impress of her nipples. I wondered whether she would kneel down to pray or slip straight into bed. She lay there in the dark, on her back, as if dead, and listened to the sounds of the other students, the flush of a toilet, the ringing of a telephone in the corridor, and then a voice calling out someone's name, and after that another voice, just a murmur, and maybe music or traffic from outside. She lay there awake, thinking of me thinking of her. The thought made me strangely happy. It was as though we were guarding each other in a world full of strangeness and danger.

The next day I went on working. I didn't answer the telephone, I already had half a dozen messages on the machine. There was Sonia, telling me her presentation had gone really well, and wishing me good luck for Thursday; there was Rüdiger, Ferdy, my mother, all of them wishing me good luck.

The day before the examination I had worked long into the night on my new project. On Thursday morning I got up early and took a last look at my old blueprint, which I would have to defend in a few hours' time; it didn't look possible to me.

On the way to the train, I saw a kite being attacked by a crow. The bird of prey was calmly tracing its circles, while the crow flapped around, then climbed higher and dropped onto the larger bird. With a minimal adjustment of its tail the kite altered its course. I stood there fascinated for a long time, watching. One time the kite appeared to give up, headed off in a different direction, and disappeared behind some trees, but then it was back again, and the crow continued to harass it. What have I got to be afraid of, I thought, it's just an exam. If worst comes to worst, I'll just have to retake it next year.

I was glad I had an early slot. It was still cool in the hall and there was hardly anyone there. Sonia had offered to come, but I said I'd rather she didn't, she would only make me nervous. In one of the rows at the back I saw my parents. They waved to me when I walked down to the front.

During the presentation I stumbled once or twice and mixed things up; I spoke of my debt to Aldo Rossi, as if that might take the wind out of the sails of my critics. To my surprise, the first expert on the panel expressed a fairly positive view of my work, even if, as he said, my debt to certain models was pretty obvious. The second examiner spent a long time on one detail, the staircases, which in his view were too narrow, but he closed with a few words praising the overall design. The other professors declined to comment, I had the feeling either they were bored or they were saving themselves for the students who were following me. After a quarter of an hour it was all over, and I left the room, followed by a couple of assistants who carried out the presentation table with my blueprints and model. The next candidates were already lining up outside, among them Rüdiger. There was a gleam in his eyes that made him look drugged. I patted him on the back and wished him good luck. He smiled uncertainly and said nothing.

My parents came out of the hall shortly after I did. They stood off to the side, beaming with pride. I talked to some other students for a bit, and then I went and joined them. That seemed to go all right, said my father, with a questioning rise in his voice, and my mother nodded, even though I was sure she couldn't have understood the half of what was said. Unlike me, they had dressed up, and they insisted on taking me out to lunch. I could feel their uncertainty. They seemed much older to me here than when I saw them at home in the familiar surroundings, and I felt a bit sorry for them. We went to a moderately priced restaurant. When we said good-bye after lunch, all three of us seemed relieved somehow to have gotten through it.

On Friday I got my grade, 2.0, which was better than I'd expected. Ferdy got the same, Sonia got a 1.0, while

Rüdiger had lost his way in the course of his presentation, and when he realized, petitioned the committee to retake his finals next year, which had been granted.

The evening after we received our grades, there was a great big party. We danced into the wee hours, and I had much too much to drink. It was getting light already as I crawled home. For a long time I was unable to sleep, all sorts of things were racing through my head; I was relieved and at the same time felt apprehensive. From now on no one was going to tell me what I had to do and what not. I thought about my new blueprint. It must be possible to create space that would allow feelings, that would enable and commu- nicate the sort of freedom and openness I was thinking of. I envisaged lofty transparent halls, open staircases, the play of light and shade. I wasn't quite sure whether I was awake or dreaming, but all at once I saw everything before me, very clear and distinct.

I woke up in the early afternoon, still reeling from so much alcohol. I hadn't said I would show up to Rüdiger's party, and come evening I dithered over whether to go or not. I didn't feel that great, and I was afraid I'd run into Alice. In the end I went.

Rüdiger's parents had a house in Possenhofen, right on Lake Starnberg. His father was a business lawyer who worked in the automobile industry; so far as I knew his grandfather already had had money. Rüdiger never boasted about how well off his family were, but you could feel it in the casual way he treated people and objects. At the time I was impressed; later on I felt sorry for him.

When I arrived, the sun was already low in the sky, and Rüdiger was just lighting some wax tapers that were dotted around the garden. He greeted me exuberantly. Hey, haven't seen you in ages, he said, thumping me on the back. He seemed perfectly relaxed, even though he was the only one of us who'd been tripped up in the exams. On the lawn between the house and the lake was a long trestle table with a white cloth, but the guests were down on the shore, a few still in the water. If you want a swim, you'd better get a move on, said Rüdiger, I'm just starting the grill. He left me, and I looked out to the others. I had the sun behind me, and everything was gleaming darkly. The scene overpowered me with a sort of timeless meditative quality it had. There was actually someone playing a guitar, and if it hadn't all been so exquisite, it would have seemed preposterous. I strolled down to the water's edge and was greeted by cheers. Sonia was lying on a blanket on the grass, she held out her hand to me and I pulled her up. She was wearing a white swimsuit with a light blue man's shirt thrown over it. She hugged me, and kissed me on both cheeks, more warmly than usual, I got the feeling. With her hand still resting on my shoulder, she whispered into my ear, look, and nodded her head to the side. Only then did I see Alice, with her head pillowed on Ferdy's belly. He was toying with her bikini top.

Those two?, I asked. Do you feel bad?, Sonia asked, and took me by the hand. Come on, let's go for a walk. At first I didn't know what she meant. It didn't feel bad at all to see Alice with Ferdy, quite the opposite, I was glad she had someone. Even if I didn't think Ferdy was right for her. I had been anxious about seeing Alice, been afraid of her sad face and her reproachful looks. Now I felt relieved. I walked through the grounds with Sonia, and she told me the story of how Alice and Ferdy had gotten together. That old pimp Rüdiger had a part in it. He brought you and her together too, remember. I never noticed, I said. Anyway, I'm glad she's not alone anymore. Me too, said Sonia, and she looped her arm through mine. Now we just need to find someone for you. And for you, I said. Sonia laughed and shook her head. I don't have time for things like that. I said I didn't believe a word of it, and she laughed again, and lowered her eyes, as though she'd spotted something in the grass. Are you all right?, she asked. Yes, I said, I think I am.

Rüdiger came out of the house carrying an enormous platter of meat, followed by his mother carrying a basket full of rolls. Sonia ran over to them and asked if she could help, and the three went back into the house. I imagined what it would be like, being here with Ivona. She would sit around stolidly, and not open her mouth, or just say bland things, like in the English Garden. I would feel ashamed by her, that was for sure. Even the notion of being alone with her by the lakeside had nothing really tempting about it. Ivona bored me, we had nothing to say to each other. It was only in bed that I liked being with her, when she lay there heavy and soft in her ugly clothes, and I felt completely free and uninhibited.

The buffet was ready. Rüdiger's mother stood in front of it. She had her hand up shielding her eyes, looking into the sun and in my direction. She waved to me, and I went to her, and she greeted me with a faint kiss on the cheek. How nice of you to come, she said. I've missed you.

I didn't know her well, but even the last time I was here, I'd been struck by her warm and easygoing nature. Don't worry, she said, I'll leave you to yourselves soon enough. Stay and eat with us, Mom, said Rüdiger. She laughed and shook her head. I'll go to bed early. I just wanted to say hello to this young man here.

She asked me a couple of questions regarding my blueprint, and listened attentively when I told her about the revised version I'd begun, and made a couple of remarks that I thought made a lot of sense. Why don't you do mine for me, said Rüdiger. Rüdiger's mother said she had studied art history. She had always had a soft spot for architecture. Back then after the war, so many heinous things had been perpetrated. Then she went back inside, and Rüdiger called the others and put steaks and sausages on the grill.

We were a small group, just over a dozen men and women. Half of us had studied with Rüdiger, Alice and one of her friends were attending the conservatory, one of Rüdiger's friends was just embarking on a career in the diplomatic service. There was Birgit, a med student, who shared an apartment with Sonia and another woman. I had seen her once or twice when I'd visited Sonia, but never exchanged more than a few words with her. A few of the guests I didn't know at all. One of them was a veterinarian, there was something agricultural about him, he didn't speak much and put away astonishing quantities of meat.

Rüdiger had drawn up a seating chart, and pointed us to our chairs. Obviously he'd been sure I would come. I was between Sonia and a woman I didn't know. Ferdy and Alice sat at the other end of the table. When I ran into Ferdy at the buffet, he seemed to think he owed me an explanation. You're not mad at me, are you?, he said. I shook my head and looked astonished. Why should I be? I'm glad she's in good hands. He grinned and raised his hands, and waggled his fingers. How's your little Polska chick? I pretended not to know what he was talking about. Did you have your foul way with her? I said I didn't know what he meant, and went back to my seat. Ferdy's remark had spoiled my mood. Everything felt artificial to me, the conversations of the others bored me, their big ideas, Ferdy's bullshit about Deconstructivism and the suppressed impurity of form. He had always been better at talking than drawing, and he changed his idols like other people changed their shirts. One day Gehry was the greatest, the next it was Libeskind or Koolhaas. His drafts changed accordingly, they had no individual idiom, they were tame, popularized versions of others' great ideas. He was bound to be successful, and make a lot of money running up second-class buildings in medium-sized cities, which his employers would take for great architecture.

Sonia started to argue with him. She worshipped Le Corbusier and loathed Deconstructivism. She talked about machines for living, and social function zones. Her naive love of the lower class must have something to do with her bourgeois background, I said. I saw that I'd offended her, but I didn't care. Rüdiger took little part in the discussion. He was probably the most gifted, certainly the most imaginative among us, only he could have failed so spectacularly. His ideas were striking and completely original, but he didn't have the energy to think them through, or if he did, he was so sloppy that the teachers couldn't be blamed for giving him bad grades. Even so, they all respected him. He had "potential." Whenever there was talk of Rüdiger, you heard that. He listened to us and then made some comment that none of us understood. He tried to explain it, and made even less sense, and then finally gave up with an enchanting smile. Then, apropos of nothing, Alice launched into an account of a concert she had gone to. Her self-promotion was even more pitiful than that of the others, she talked with a kind of artificial gush and showed off like a little girl. All the people she met were geniuses, all the books she read were masterpieces, all the music she heard or played was fantastic.

After a while I couldn't stand any more of her nonsense, and I went down to the lake. On either side of the swimming spot were old trees, which looked like living beings in the flickering light of the torches. I could make out the lights on the opposite side, glinting and multiplying on the surfaces of the water. I lit a cigarette, and heard footsteps behind me. It was the veterinary med student. He was holding a sausage in one hand; with his mouth full, he said, we haven't met yet, and held out his other hand. His name was Jakob. He had a strong regional accent, and said he was from some place in the Bayerischer Wald, called Oberkashof. Had I come across it? It wouldn't be anywhere near Unterkashof, I asked, and he laughed deafeningly and smacked me on the back. You'll do, he said. Then he started raving about Sonia, whom he called an attractive hussy. I don't know how he got onto the subject of folkloric costume, and how he thought the dirndl was the perfect garment for the female body. It supported the bosom and emphasized the waist, and covered the less pleasing aspect of the hips. Imagine Sonia in a dirndl, he said lasciviously. I had to laugh. Suddenly he was talking about eunuchs. Early and late castrates, family eunuchoidism, reeds and silver tubes and Chinese castration chairs with slanted armrests. A eunuch's physique was distorted by the absence of male

44

hormones and the disrupted assimilation of protein. I said
I would get myself something to drink.

When I passed the table, I heard Alice talking about the
death of Karajan. He had managed to conduct one rehearsal
of *Un ballo in maschera*, she said, her voice growing shrill.
She shook her head and rolled her eyes like a lunatic.

Lass uns ihn gerettet sehen, ew'ger Gott!
O lass uns ihn, lass uns ihn gerettet sehn!
Er stirbt!—Er stirbt!—
*O grauenvolle Nacht!**

I took the subway back into the city with Sonia. As I said
good-bye to Rüdiger, he had asked me about Ivona too.
I motioned dismissively with my hand, that business was
embarrassing to me, not least with Sonia standing next to
me. On the train she started asking me about her. Wow, she
said, with an ironic smile, a Polish girl, eh. It's nothing, I
said, Ferdy talked to her, and then we couldn't get rid of
her all evening. Poles are spirited women, said Sonia, you
should watch yourself. You should see her, I said, she's not
attractive, she's boring, she doesn't talk, and if she does
say something it's just a platitude. Sonia looked at me in

* Let us see him safe, Almighty God! / Let us see him safe and well! /
He dies!—He dies!— / O dreadful night!

45

surprise. Don't be so defensive. And anyway, she's a devout Catholic, I added. The woman doesn't interest me, is that so hard to understand? But you walked her home. That was politeness. The way you talk about her isn't especially polite. I rolled my eyes. When women get sisterly with each other, it's best not to say anything. Sonia didn't speak for a while either. She seemed to be thinking. Then she said she was going to Marseilles the following week, to see Le Corbusier's Cité Radieuse, and would I like to go with her. She was going to drive there, and we could stay with a friend of hers, a German painter who lived in the city, on account of the light.

I thought a couple of days off would do me good after the stresses of the exam, and the trip wouldn't cost much. Maybe I would finally be able to shake off Ivona if I went. I wouldn't have to be thinking about her all the time if I was with Sonia. Sure, I said, I'd like that. Even though it's not my scene. Sonia laughed. I know you don't like any other architect except yourself, that's the presumption of genius. I looked at her with mock condescension. I knew she was making fun of me, but even so I liked it when she called me a genius.

We were going to leave on Monday. If we set off early, Sonia said, then we could do the drive in a day. So I just had Sunday to make my preparations. I got up early and went to the laundromat, which was in the basement of one of the buildings. When I stepped outside my house, I looked around. I was probably scared Ivona would get wind of my plans. I felt I was betraying her in getting ready to go on a trip with another girl. There was no one to be seen. I didn't think Ivona knew where I lived. She was probably in church, busy praying for me. That threw me into a rage, and for a moment I thought of sending her a note telling her to leave me alone, and that I never wanted to see her again. But what could I hold against her? It wasn't her doing that I had to think about her all the time, that she had some power over me, a thought that simultaneously fascinated and infuriated me. I was almost certain her hold would only last as long as she kept me at a distance. If I really wanted to get free I would have to sleep with her.

I put the laundry in a washer and slid in the coins. Back in the bungalow, it was baking hot. I lay down on the bed and stared up at the ceiling. I was in the sort of feverish mood I often got into when there was a trip ahead, and I couldn't face doing anything, and could only sit around and wait. Maybe that was why I got further and further into something till I couldn't think straight anymore.

I walked rapidly through the almost empty streets, where the heat bounced off the pavement and walls. I broke into a sweat, and the few sounds I heard reached me as though through a filter. The thought churned around and around in my brain, I've got to have her, I kept thinking, she wants

47

it too, she's waiting for me. Outside the student residence, I
stood under the projecting shade of the roof for a moment.
My T-shirt was sweated through, and I was out of breath
from walking so fast. I could still turn back, I thought, and
nothing would have changed. For one disembodied moment, time seemed to stand still, but it wasn't hesitation,
it was more the moment at the start of a race, a moment
of maximum stillness and absolute concentration. Then I
saw my finger press Ivona's bell, and I imagined I could
hear the shrill of it tearing the silence. A minute later, I
saw Ivona through the glass door as she came downstairs.
She was wearing a dark blue skirt and a white blouse, her
church clothes, I guessed, her Sunday best. When she saw
me, she paused for a moment, then hurriedly took the
remaining steps and unlocked the door. I took her hand,
and she stood there, twisting a little, something that would
have been appropriate in a little girl but looked ridiculous
when she did it. I followed her upstairs and into her room.
I was still very calm, but Ivona must have sensed there was
something amiss. She backed up toward the window, and
I followed her. This time she didn't turn to the bed, but
stayed where she was. I started to unbutton her blouse. She
placed her hands over mine, and held them, but I freed
myself with a sudden movement. I took off her blouse and
her skirt, slip and tights, which she wore in spite of the
heat. At first she resisted a bit, but I was the stronger, and
eventually she gave up any resistance. When I pulled down

her panties, she said, no, but she stepped out of them, first one foot then the other. She stood there awkwardly, both feet on the floor, and trying to cover herself up, but I held her hands and knelt down in front of her, kissing her. Her white untouched flesh had something vegetable about it, the pleats in her skin which was thickly sown with moles, her black, crisp pubic hair. I was almost beside myself with lust. Then she turned around and took another step forward to the window, so that she could have been seen from the street. I got up and, while I quickly stripped, looked outside with her. There was no one in sight, no witness, I thought. Come, I said, and made to pull her over to the bed. Then she started crying. Her crying got more and more violent, until her whole body was cramped up and shaking. She collapsed into herself, and sat hunkered on the floor, still crying softly. It was as though I woke up. I sat down on the bed and stared at her. I remember something Aldo Rossi had said, that every room contains an abyss. The abyss was between me and Ivona. I stretched out my hand to hold her, and hold her to me, but she shrank back. She looked deep into my eyes, her expression was full of fear and sadness. I quickly got dressed and left.

That's not a nice story, said Antje. Her voice sounded low and serious. I know, I said, and you're the first person I've told it to. Why me?

Instead of taking the road via Traubing as I usually did, I drove along the lakefront, even though it was night, and there wasn't much to see. There was a time I was bored by this landscape, but the longer I lived here, the more I saw its beauty. Sometimes, when Sonia was in bed already, I would go for a walk down to the Academy, and sit by the shore and think about my life, and how it could have been different. Then I would have the feeling it had all happened automatically, without any input from me, as though it had to be this way. I admired people like Antje who seemed to have their lives in their hands, and set themselves goals, and made decisions.

I parked outside the house, but Antje made no move. I don't really feel like going in there with you, she said quietly. It's almost twenty years ago, I said. You're sitting here in your house, with your beautiful wife and your sweet little girl. Don't you feel any shame? I haven't gotten to the end of the story yet, I said. Well, I've heard enough for today, said Antje, and she climbed out.

I showed her to the guest bedroom, which was right beside the front door, and facing the office on the lower ground floor. Sonia had everything ready. There were towels laid out on the freshly made bed and flowers on the table by the window. She had even written a welcome card and propped it against the vase. Antje read it and set it down with a smile. Mathilda, our cat, walked in. Sophie had been pestering us for ages, and finally for her tenth birthday she was allowed to have the kitten her grandparents had promised her long before. But now, half a year later, her interest had let up noticeably, and we continually needed to remind her to look after her pet. Mathilda strolled through my legs and looked up at Antje, who was taking her toiletries from her overnight bag. You have your own bathroom, I said, here on the right. Will you remove the cat, please?, said Antje. I asked her if she didn't like animals. I like wild animals, not pets.

I said good night and turned to leave. Wait, said Antje, and dropped onto her bed. You didn't answer my question. Why tell me all this? We hardly know each other. Maybe that's the reason, I said. Do you remember when you showed me your paintings back then? Antje made a doubtful face. You didn't like them. Actually, no one liked them, not even me. You said I was too young for them, I said, but that wasn't true. I recognized myself in your copulating chimeras. I felt trapped, maybe that's why I didn't want to see your pictures. Aren't you making things a teeny bit simple for yourself?, asked Antje. You behave like a swine, and then you blame your inner beast. I'm not buying that. Maybe I thought, because you're an artist, you'd understand, I said. Antje stopped to think. She had some understanding for craziness, but she couldn't understand what I'd done. You had to be able to tell the difference between fiction and reality. Imagine someone doing that to your daughter. I said that wasn't fair, Sophie was still a child. That's not the point, said Antje.

Finally we said good night, and I went upstairs to Sophie's room. The only light was from a small blue night-light, in which Sophie's face looked very calm. While I gazed at her, she quickly furrowed her brow, and I wondered what was going on in her head, what she could have been dreaming about. Sometimes she came into our room, I would wake up for some reason to find her standing by our bed and staring at me with a frightened expression. When I sent her back she would say she'd had a bad dream. Then she would tell exotic stories about wild animals and wicked men, and sometimes great big destructive machines, and I would tell her to try and think of something else, something pretty. I can't, she would say.

I went into the bathroom and got changed. When I lay down, Sonia woke briefly, gave me a kiss, and went straight back to sleep. I thought of the pictures I'd taken of her asleep, and that she'd seen later. That was the first time we'd kissed, on that little island in front of the port at Marseilles. It all seemed terribly long ago.

When I got to the parking lot, Sonia was already there. She got out, said hello, and opened the trunk. There was hardly any room for my duffle bag next to her huge wheeled suitcase. I asked her what she'd packed, I'd thought we were only going for a couple of days. Things I need, she said, and a few books and my Rolleiflex. Did you bring a camera? I don't need a camera, I've got eyes in my head and a good memory. You're just lazy, Sonia said.

It was a cool morning, everything felt clean and fresh. It was due to get hot again by noon, but by then we'd be in the mountains, Sonia promised. She'd thought of everything, she had all the necessary maps with her, and water and a thermos of coffee. Some sandwiches were in a picnic basket on the back seat. We're going to go via the San Bernardino Pass, said Sonia, past Milan and along the Ligurian coast. It's a pretty route. I said I'd be glad to take turns driving. We'll see, she said.

It really was a lovely drive. We had never spent so much time together, and we got on like a house on fire. Sonia talked about Le Corbusier, she knew everything about him and his work. She asked me what I had against him. Nothing, I said, I just don't like him. There's something conceited about his buildings. I always get the feeling they're out to turn me into an ideal man. Have you ever been inside any of his buildings? No, I said, but I've seen loads of pictures. Sonia said, pictures weren't enough, the essence of Le Corbusier wasn't in the facades, but in the rooms. Anyway, what could be bad about a building that improved the people who lived in it? I said, people have a history that you have to respect. Attempts to create a better man were at best misguided and at worst had led to atrocious crimes. What did Le Corbusier do in the war, by the way? Sonia said she wasn't exactly sure, but he certainly hadn't been a fascist. In twenty years' time no one will speak about Deconstructivism anymore, but Le Corbusier will still be around.

Later we talked about our final projects, and when I told Sonia I'd started mine all over again, she looked at me in amazement. I told her about my new ideas. That the structure should emerge from the paths and grow, like a plant, that the halls shouldn't just be the empty space between walls, but atmospheric bodies, sculptures of light and shade. While I spoke, I got the feeling I hadn't done so badly over the last week. Of course it's a waste of time, now that I've got my degree in my pocket. Sonia asked me if I'd like to work with her on the day-care design for the contest. That surprised me, because a day or two earlier she'd rejected all my suggestions, and basically we had completely different ideas about architecture. Do you really think we'd make a good team? You make a more interesting class of mistake, said Sonia, and laughed.

At lunchtime we were at the pass. We parked the car and ate our sandwiches. Then we lay in the sun, until Sonia said we'd better get going. I asked if she wanted me to take over, but she shook her head, maybe later, she didn't feel tired yet. I wasn't too unhappy about that, because I wasn't an experienced driver, and I enjoyed sitting idly next to Sonia and staring out the window at the passing scenery.

Somehow we came to speak about Rüdiger. I asked Sonia why she'd broken up with him. He broke up with me. That I don't understand, I said, how anyone could leave a woman like you. Sonia quickly turned to look at me, and smiled ironically. Tell him that.

They had been together since high school, she said, and had grown up only a mile or two apart. Rüdiger had decided to go into architecture for her sake. He could just as well have done something completely different. You know him, he can do anything and does nothing.

When she started university, Sonia had found a room in a communal apartment, but Rüdiger continued to travel into the city from his parents' house at Possenhofen every day. We had a good time, but it bugged me that he was still at his parents'. But his mother's nice, I said. Yes, she is, and so's his father too, but Rüdiger somehow can't get free of them. Eventually I gave him an ultimatum. He decided in favor of his parents. Sonia laughed. She could easily imagine Rüdiger never getting married, he wasn't really interested in women. Do you think he's gay? No, said Sonia, he's not interested in men either. What's left? She shrugged her shoulders. I don't know. She said she didn't hold anything against Rüdiger, quite the contrary, at seventeen she'd been quite relieved to have a boyfriend who wasn't pressuring her into this and that. I didn't respond. It's the same with work, said Sonia, perhaps that bothered me more. He's just got no energy. It's typical of him to have bailed before his final. Now he can go on being a student for another year. I wouldn't be surprised if he never receives his degree.

We were out of the mountains and crossing a huge flat plain. The nearer we got to Milan, the denser the traffic. Sonia was silent now, she had to concentrate. Then we were in open country again, and the traffic was lighter. What do you look to a woman for?, she asked. I don't look for anything in particular. When I've fallen in love with her, I just have to take her the way she is. Sonia laughed. I must be a hopeless romantic. That's why women have to be sensible and choose their men. Is that what you do?, I asked. She didn't say anything for a moment, and then she replied, sure I do that.

The air was hazy, and the car got very hot. We rolled the windows down and listened to the radio, and then later to cassettes. Every so often I would offer to take over the driving, but each time she shook her head and said, I can do it. Two or three times she stopped, without consulting me, at a service station, and we drank lukewarm coffee from the thermos, and peed, and then we drove on.

It was late afternoon when we got to the coast, and about an hour later we were in France. Not much farther now, said Sonia.

We reached Marseilles at eight in the evening, after driving for twelve hours. Unfortunately it took us another half an hour to find the house where Sonia's friend lived. It wasn't far from the old harbor, but the quarter was a tangle of one-way streets, and we drove around in endless circles, sometimes following signs to CENTRE VILLE, and sometimes TOUTES DIRECTIONS. Isn't that great, I said, wherever you want to get to there's only one way. Sonia didn't say anything. She looked tired and stressed out.

Finally we found the house, a five-story Art Nouveau building with a grimy facade, and not too far away from it, an empty parking spot. Sonia switched the engine off and sat still. She said she was a bit tired now. Shall I carry you upstairs? She said Antje lived on the fifth floor.

Sonia went ahead while I lugged her suitcase and my bag up the steps. Above me I could hear the two friends greeting each other. This is Alexander, said Sonia, once I reached the door, and this is Antje. Alex, I said, and shook hands with the painter. She wore capri pants and a sleeveless top. Her hair was as blond as Sonia's. She had small strong hands and must have been quite a bit older than us, around forty, I guessed.

So did you manage to snaffle him after all?, she said with a naughty grin. Antje!, cried Sonia with a show of horror, and laughed. We're just buddies, as you know perfectly well. Antje asked us in, she had some food ready. She led the way down a dark hallway. From the outside, the building had looked a bit dilapidated, but the apartment was in a good state, the rooms were bright and had high ceilings and old creaky floorboards. The walls were covered with small old paintings of animals, meerkats and birds, ungulates and rodents. There was something disturbing about them, they were eerie and seemed to be observing us, lying in wait. Antje led the way out onto the balcony, and a table laid with bread and cheese, raw ham, olives, and a large bowl of salad, all in the light of an oil lamp and a few candles.

We ate and drank wine and talked. At eleven, Antje asked us if we felt like going out, but Sonia said she was dog tired. You can choose, said Antje, either you can sleep with your nice buddy in the guest room, or you can share the master bed with me. Sonia was sheepish, I hadn't seen that in her before, it was quite moving. After her brief hesitation, she said, I'll sleep with you. That's what I was afraid of, said Antje. Come on, I'll show you the room. The two women disappeared together. I stayed on the balcony, looking down onto the street, from where there was noisy shouting. A delivery truck was in the middle of the road and the driver of a car was leaning out of the window cursing the truck driver, who was taking all the time in the world to unload some large boxes and pile them up on the sidewalk.

Sonia says to wish you a good night, said Antje, when she came back. Do you mind if I have a cigarette? I asked if the paintings in the apartment were all by her. There was something disconcerting about them. Come, said Antje, and she took a couple of hurried drags, and put out her cigarette. She took me into the sitting room and switched on the light. Look at them closely. Once again I had the feeling I was being watched, but it took me a while to understand the cause of it. The animals had human eyes. I'll show you my new ones, said Antje. She led me to a large room at the end of the hallway. The parquet floor was covered by large pieces of cardboard, on the walls were a few dark pictures, but in the half-light it was difficult to make out what they were. Antje walked through the room and bent down. A construction light on a tripod flared up, so bright that for a moment I was dazzled. Then I saw the strange beings in the paintings, a man with a fish head and an enormous cock he was holding in both hands, a bull mounting a cow, both with human heads, two dogs with human privates, licking each other. In the background were sketched in cityscapes, half-decayed high-rise apartments, deserted pedestrian walkways, a gray industrial park. The paintings were done in oil, in dark shades, and they had something old masterly about them. The one of the two dogs was still unfinished, the background was just outlined in charcoal on the primed canvas. I didn't know what to say. I didn't find the paintings beautiful, they were even more disquieting than the small ones in the other rooms, but they were undeniably powerful and unsettling. They didn't seem to me to go with my idea of Antje, who in her conversation was pretty conventional, the way she talked to Sonia about clothes and going out and Munich compared to Marseilles. Antje didn't seem to be interested at all in my opinion. Welcome to the zoo, she said with a mocking expression. She unplugged the light, and it was dark, but a different dark now that I knew what terrifying beings were concealed in it. We went back out to the balcony. Antje filled our glasses and looked at me directly. The silence was difficult, I had the feeling I had to say something. You're unsettling. Yes, said Antje. It wasn't a confirmation, more a sort of prompt, as though expecting me to carry on. I felt as if I was being tested. What's the name of the painter who did *The Garden of Earthly Delights*? That's what it reminds me of. Don't trouble yourself, said Antje. Sonia doesn't like them either. Perhaps you're both just too young and cosseted. She asked me what my animal was. I thought about it, but I couldn't think of one. A bird?, I suggested. That's what they all say. Antje shook her head. A gazelle. That would fit Sonia better than me, I said. Antje twisted her mouth. No, Sonia is domesticated. She's a sheep, or maybe a guinea pig, yes, that's right, a guinea pig. I laughed. You're not very nice, are you. I'm most like a dog, said Antje, a stray dog, that's not very flattering either. I wondered what sort of animal Ivona might be. Perhaps a dog as well, I thought, but Ivona wasn't domesticated, under her quiet, long-suffering manner there was still something wild, a resolve that I'd rarely come across in a human being.

And how do you like your guinea pig?, asked Antje. We're just classmates, I said. At the most, we might enter a competition together one day. Didn't you notice that Sonia wants more from you? I shook my head. She's got no time for a relationship. And you believe her when she says that?, asked Antje with an ambiguous smile. I don't think she's in love with me. Nor do I, said Antje. It would be wrong to expect too much of her.

We went on drinking and talking. Antje seemed to get a kick out of unsettling me. Her boyfriend lived in Munich, she said, and that was fine by her. She couldn't stand having a man around her all the time, it would interfere with her work. I expect you want to get married and start a family? I don't know, I said. If you want to get married, Sonia's the perfect wife. She's beautiful, intelligent, cultivated, and she's a good sort. That's not enough, I said. I don't think you're cut out for a great love, said Antje. Nor am I, by the way, either.

She had only really fallen in love once, she said, when she was twenty, with a man fifteen years older. Georg was Antje's teacher at art school. He lived in Hamburg, and only traveled down to Munich every other week, to look at his students' work. He had a wife and four children, as he'd told Antje right at the start. To begin with, their relationship wasn't much more than an affair.

But then over time I got to become more and more of a second wife to him, said Antje, he took me along to openings, introduced me to important people, and helped to find me a gallery. She was the only student who had had a gallery before she graduated. She liked being the lover of a prominent painter, and Georg had treated her well, taking her to expensive restaurants and giving her presents.

After graduation, Antje fell into a hole, she couldn't deal with her newly won freedom, and had no more ideas. She worked like a lunatic and got nowhere. Georg was her last connection to the art scene. When he came to Munich, she perked up for a few days, touring the galleries with him, staying up all night. But he had new students, young talents, who were more of an inspiration to him than she was. I was just the one he fucked, she said. The more Georg turned away from her, the more she clung to him. She was getting nowhere with her painting, so she devoted all her energies to jealousy.

He had one very talented student, said Antje, I don't think there was anything between them, but I couldn't think straight anymore. I trailed him from the Academy once, and followed him when he went out drinking with his class. I sat down at the next table, so he could see me. Then I wrote him interminable letters, embarrassing letters, I hope to God he's thrown them away. Sometimes I was aggressive, sometimes submissive, sometimes both at the same time. I'd call him at home in Hamburg, until he changed his number. He threatened he would end my career. I was besotted with him, that's the only way I can describe it. I had physical symptoms, migraine attacks, stomach cramps. Once when I saw him going to an opening with that student I mentioned, I spent the night puking. At four a.m. I called his hotel. Of course the night receptionist didn't put me through. I was sure Georg was with the new student. It never crossed my mind that he might just be sleeping.

I can laugh about it now, said Antje, but at the time I was on the verge of insanity. When it was over I swore I would never fall in love like that again. And I stuck to it. Whatever the novels say, *amour fou* is an inferior form of love. If a cultivated person starts acting like a madman, that is humiliating and a sign of immaturity. She filled our glasses. Those are stories that everyone enjoys listening to, but if they happen to you, you just wish it would end. She asked me what I had to find fault with in Sonia. Nothing. She likes you, said Antje. When she called to tell me that you were coming, she raved about you. I asked her if you two were an item. No, she said, not yet.

I emptied my glass and said I was tired and was going to bed. Come on, said Antje, and she took my arm. Her voice wasn't slurred or anything, but I could tell by her movements that she was drunk. She showed me the guest room and bathroom. Outside her bedroom, she pressed her finger to her lips and took my hand. She opened the door softly and led me up to the bed. I had never seen Sonia asleep before. While I looked at her, something strange happened. Her features seemed to change, it was as though I was seeing the face of the old woman she would one day become. Antje bent down over her, kissed her on the brow, and said, good night, little guinea pig.

The next morning, when I came into the kitchen, Sonia and Antje were already sitting there, drinking coffee. They stopped talking and smiled. I was sure they'd been talking about me. Antje stood up to get me a cup. Sonia called me a sleepyhead.

After breakfast we went to the Cité Radieuse and had a tour of that rather run-down building. Sonia pointed out every detail to me, and tiptoed down the dark corridors, as though we were in a church. She was right—only now that I was actually inside the building did I notice its quality. The rooms and stairwells were surprisingly small, and even though the building was eighteen stories high, because it was supported on concrete pillars it seemed extraordinarily light. It was the first building Le Corbusier had built using the Modulor, his invented system of measurements, Sonia told me. I vaguely remembered it coming up at school. Sonia showed me an illustration from her guidebook, a muscular, asexual being with big hands and small head, and a hole in place of its navel. Does he live here then?, I asked. The ideal inhabitant of the ideal house.

We took the elevator up to the roof terrace. Up there it was hot, and I sat down in the shade of the superstructure and read the guidebook while Sonia scouted everything.

We took the bus back into the city. Sonia's eyes were shining, and she was enthusing about the "unit for living." There was no sense that we'd just seen it together. The building had impressed me, but I felt like contradicting Sonia. Be honest, would you want to live there? In a second she said, wouldn't you? I'm not sure, machine for living, I mean, the very expression. You might as well say battery farm. The individuality comes through the inhabitants, said Sonia, the building is just a container. My critique seemed to annoy her. Her face was a little flushed, which suited her. Shall we go to the sea?, I asked. Maybe later, she said, I'd like to jot down a few notes first.

Antje had gone out. She wasn't going to be back until tonight, she said at breakfast. We had a bite to eat from the fridge, and then Sonia disappeared into Antje's room, and I took a seat in the living room and browsed through some coffee-table books about animals that I found on the sofa. In Brehm's animal encyclopedia I read the article about guinea pigs. According to Brehm, they were easy to keep, harmless, cheerful, and undemanding. If you just gave them something to eat, they'd be happy pretty much anywhere. On the other hand, they weren't truly affectionate, just friendly to anyone who treated them well.

It was hot in the apartment, but a breeze came in through the open balcony door carrying the sounds of the city, which sounded surprisingly near. I stretched out on the sofa and imagined what it would be like to live with Sonia in the Cité Radieuse. We would have two kids, a girl and a boy. We would eat breakfast as a family, and then take the children downstairs to the day care, and go to our studio, where we both worked on social housing projects. It was an open, brightly lit space in the city center, with large tables with blueprints on them, and white cardboard models of machines for living scattered about. Then we went on site. Sonia looked lovely in beige pants and a white linen shirt and white plastic helmet. Huge red cranes stood around, but no one seemed to be working. The sky was blue, and you could see the sea in the distance and sense the nearness of Africa just across the water. It was a scene from a French movie of the fifties or sixties, our whole life was a film put together from distance shots, wide angles under white light, with little people moving through it, all very aesthetic and intellectual and cool.

I got up and went out into the hallway. I knocked gently on the door of Antje's room and said quietly, Sonia? No reply. The door was half-open, and I went inside. Sonia was lying on the bed asleep, one arm curled over her head on the pillow. There was a small dark sweat stain in her armpit, the one flaw in an otherwise perfect picture. I stroked it with my finger, I didn't dare any other touch. The Rolleiflex was on the desk. I picked it up and started to take pictures of Sonia. The image in the frame was reversed, and it took me a while to get used to the fact that every move I made had the reverse effect. Slowly I circled the bed, looking for the perfect setup, moving in and then back again. I took a couple of shots, once, when I was really near, Sonia's brow creased at the sound of the shutter, and I was afraid she'd wake up, but her face relaxed again, and I went on taking pictures. Then the film was full, and I took it out, sealed it, and laid it with the other rolls that Sonia had shot that morning. As I was about to leave the room, I heard Sonia's drowsy voice call my name. I turned around and went back to her. I must have gone to sleep, she said. I said I'd dozed off as well.

Sonia said she was going to take the films to be developed, would I like to go with her. We went to the photo shop down the street and then we had a drink in a bistro in the old harbor.

The next day Sonia wanted to take a look at the Château d'If. Antje had told us that boats went from there to a couple of small islands where you could bathe in the sea. We packed our swimming things, bought a few sandwiches, and picked up the prints in the photo shop.

The boat left from the old harbor. Even though it was early in the morning, bathers thronged the jetty. When the ship left port, it crossed various little fishing boats and farther out an enormous ferry that was probably coming from Corsica or from North Africa. The light and the salt smell and the ships reminded me of family holidays, and I felt a bit like I used to then, at once lost and full of expectation.

Not many passengers got off at the Château d'If, most of them were staying on till the bathing islands. The fortress fascinated me right away with its monumentality and its deployment of simple forms. It consisted of a quadratic central structure, with three massive towers at the corners. It had been built five hundred years ago, and had been used, almost from the start, as a prison. The central keep had a small inner courtyard with a well and galleries, from which you gained access to the cells. The cells were dark, with very little light reaching them through the narrow, low-set archery slits. Sonia said the walls were ten or twelve feet thick in places, and she began copying some of the details into her sketchbook. I tried to imagine what it would be like to be imprisoned here. Oddly, I had a sensation of shelter and protection rather than confinement.

On the castle roof, the light was dazzlingly bright and threw sharp black shadows onto the reddish stone. You could see the city in the distance, but the land was already so hazy that you could only make out the outlines of the buildings. After an hour we took the boat out to the islands. It was full of tanned young people in plastic flip-flops and bathing suits and not much more.

The ship docked at Frioul, the first of the islands. At the jetty a little train stood by to transport the visitors to the beach, but Sonia first wanted to look at the ruins of the German fort on a cliff overlooking the harbor. We climbed the rocky path. The heat was stifling, and when we got to the top, I was in a lather of sweat, and took off my T-shirt. Sonia seemed unaffected by the heat, she still looked fresh as a daisy. Paul Virilio compared these bunkers to grave sites, she said, while she walked among the ruins. He said it was as though the men went freely to their graves, to protect themselves from death. We had reached the highest point, and on the horizon there was a collection of concrete crosses. As we approached, we saw that they weren't part of some military cemetery, but supports that must once have sustained something heavy, like a roof or antiaircraft artillery. Even so, the crosses lent a sort of morbid aspect to the place. Virilio calls the bunkers temples without religion, said Sonia.

On the way downhill, she asked me if I was religious. She wasn't happy with my reply, my views were too diffuse and frivolous for her liking. You had to have a standpoint. She believed in people and humanity and progress. You're just a child of the modern age, I said, and Sonia laughed and said, that to her was a compliment. I thought of something Le Corbusier had said, that I'd seen in a vitrine in the Cité Radieuse: *Everything is different. Everything is new. Everything is beautiful.* And for a moment I thought I could believe in that.

The little beach at the foot of the hill was too crowded for us, but not far off we found a bay with fewer people. The rocks were jagged, and we searched for a while before we found a flat spot where we could spread our towels. It was sheltered, and the air carried a faint smell of mold. Fifty yards offshore a couple of yachts rode at anchor, with no one to be seen on them. I put on my swimming trunks, Sonia sat down without changing. Won't you come for a swim?, I asked. She shook her head and said she preferred swimming pools, she was afraid of jellyfish and sea urchins and various other sea creatures.

I had to clamber over some rocks to get to the water, which seemed surprisingly cool for the time of year. I swam out a few yards. Looking back, I saw Sonia taking the photograph envelopes out of her bag. I swam as far as the yachts, rounded them, and turned back. Sonia was sitting there just as before, staring out to sea. When I dropped onto the towel next to her, she took the pictures that had been in her lap and handed them to me without a word. I dried my hands and looked through them, photos of the Cité Radieuse, other buildings, and places in the inner city. Then there were the pictures I had taken of Sonia asleep. They weren't as good as I had hoped they would be, but Sonia still looked very good in them, almost like a statue. I turned to her. She had lain down and shut her eyes, it was almost as though she was imitating the pictures, but her attitude had something stiff about it. She had drawn up her legs and was pressing her knees together, and she seemed very young. I think she was waiting for me to kiss her, at any rate it didn't seem to surprise her when I did. She put her arms around my neck and pulled me down to her.

We walked hand in hand back to the jetty, not saying a word. Sometimes I stopped and pulled Sonia toward me and kissed her. My mood was a mixture of formal and light-hearted. I had thought a lot about Sonia, and she probably had about me. We hadn't kissed out of some whim, and it was clear to me from that moment on that the kiss was a decision we had come to together. On the boat back, Sonia asked me what my plans were, and whether I wanted to do a training course abroad, and later start my own architectural firm and family. We spoke lightly, but under everything there was the seriousness with which only young people talk about life. I didn't feel so much in love as happy and confident and maybe proud.

Outside the apartment Sonia kissed me again, a short, concluding kiss, as if to make it clear to me that our relationship was to be kept secret from Antje. But in the course of the evening, we gave up our discretion. We had dinner on the balcony again, and were sitting there talking about architecture and Marseilles. Sonia said she hadn't just come here for Le Corbusier. She also wanted to look for an internship. She had a couple of addresses of firms that interested her, and was going to go around and look at them. If you don't mind, she said, taking my hand. Antje raised her eyebrows and smirked. Well, at least I'll have my bed to myself tonight, she said. She looked at Sonia. Or won't I? No one said anything, and I think even Antje was a little embarrassed by the silence. Maybe Sonia and I were too well acquainted to become lovers just like that. When going swimming I had often enough changed in her presence, but now when I thought about sleeping in the same bed with her, I felt a little bashful. With a quiet, uncertain voice, she said if it was okay with Antje, she would like to stay in her room. She got up, kissed me—as if by way of compensation—quickly on the mouth, and disappeared into the apartment. After she had been gone a little while, I followed her inside. I found her in Antje's room. She was sitting on the bed, crying. I sat down next to her and put my arm around her, and asked her what the matter was. I'm so happy, she said, but I'm embarrassed. Embarrassed with me? No, silly, not you, in front of Antje. I was pretty sure she felt embarrassed in front of me as well, and maybe even with herself too. It doesn't matter, I said. We've got all the time in the world.

In the morning Sonia was the same as always. When I went into the kitchen, she was just fixing coffee. I reached around her waist and she kissed me, as though we'd been going out for years, and then she turned away and fished the milk and butter out of the fridge. Today I'm going to visit architects' studios, she said cheerfully, do you want some orange juice? I asked her if she didn't want to call ahead to set up interviews, but she shook her head. The best thing was just to drop by, once people saw you they had more trouble saying no to you. You mean your beauty will win them over? She looked at me furiously. That's mean, I can't help the way I look. I said it could be worse, and laid my hands on her shoulders and pulled her against me, and now she hugged me and kissed me properly. She asked if I'd slept well. I said, I dreamed about you. That's not true, admit it.

Sonia spent the next days traipsing around various

architect firms in Marseilles. I went with her and waited
nearby in a bistro, drank a cup of coffee, and read until she
came out. She shook her head, and before we got out the
door she unfolded her list, put a line through the entry, and
looked for the next one. So many rejections didn't seem to
affect her self-confidence in the least, she was tough, I'd
noticed that at school. Whereas I reacted aggressively to
criticism and referred to the professors as idiots, she listened carefully and tried to do better.

We were out all day, I'd already switched from coffee to
Pernod, and had stopped reading and instead just watched
the people in the cafés, when I saw Sonia emerging from
a building she'd gone into a half an hour before. A good-
looking man of middle age held the door open for her, and
the two of them walked down the street together. I paid at the
bar and followed them, but even before I'd caught up, the
man opened the door of a white minivan and showed Sonia
in. I looked for a taxi. Of course there were none to be seen.
I stood there for a while not knowing what to do, before
finally setting off back to Antje's apartment.

Antje was sitting in the living room reading. She asked
me what I'd done with Sonia. Nothing, she climbed into a
car with a man and drove off. Sounds promising, said Antje,
would you like a mint tea, I've just made some.

In the kitchen I asked Antje how she met Sonia in the
first place. She was friends with Sonia's parents, Antje said,
she'd known Sonia from when she was a little girl. Was she

like that then? Antje nodded. A bit precocious and terribly serious. She had a way about her that commanded respect, even when she was just little. Basically everyone did what she said, often without realizing it. She always seemed to be thinking of other people. It never occurred to you that it might be to her advantage too. One of my professors introduced Sonia's parents to me. They used to go to every opening back then. I had a problem with an unwanted pregnancy, and Sonia's father helped. Afterward he treated me free of charge for many years. I gave him the occasional picture by way of thanks, but I think he only took it so as not to give me the feeling of owing him. He never put any of them up on his walls, that's for sure. Maybe his wife didn't like them. He's a very cultivated man, said Antje, did you get to meet him ever? Only briefly, at an end-of-semester presentation. Sonia introduced me to both of them. But she was still going out with Rüdiger at the time. Antje laughed. She brought him to visit me once too. I was at the Villa Massimo in Rome at the time. He was classy. How do you mean? Antje shrugged her shoulders. Oh, she said, I don't know, he was something special, crazy guy. We turned Rome upside down, me and him. Sonia spent the whole day touring cultural sites and went to bed early. I asked her when that was. Last year. Antje looked at me, laughed, and said, there wasn't anything. You didn't think that, did you? No, he's not that type. We just hit it off together. But even then I sensed that their relationship was rocky.

She said she was very fond of Sonia, initially on her parents' account, but she struck her as being a bit earnest. I
recalled that Ferdy had once said Sonia was the most hu-
morless person he'd ever come across, she would ask to be
excused when she laughed. At the time I'd contradicted
him, just as I contradicted Antje now, but presumably they
were right and I wasn't.

Sonia turned up an hour later. She asked where I'd gone,
she'd been looking for me in the café. She was too excited
to be upset about my disappearance, but I was angry. I saw
you drive off with a man, I said, the least you could do was
tell me where you were going. Or are you ashamed of me? I
was standing there like a piece of trash. Sonia hugged and
kissed me. You poor thing, that was Albert, he says I can
do my internship at his firm. And I suppose you had to go
and celebrate that together right away, I said, still irritated.
He showed me a construction site, he had to go anyway and
just took me with him. I didn't know it would take so long.

Maybe Sonia did have a bad conscience after all. That
evening she was especially sweet to me. This time we went
out to eat, in a little bar in the old harbor, where Antje
claimed they served the best fish in Marseilles. We drank a
lot of wine, Sonia drank more than she usually did, and we
toasted all kinds of things, Sonia's internship, the future,
architecture, Sonia and me. Afterward we went to a club
where it was so loud that most of the time we just sat there
and looked at each other helplessly and shook our heads

and laughed. Antje ran into someone she knew and motioned to him to join us. She laughed even more than before, and put her hand on the man's thigh, and kept leaning across to him, and yelled things in his ear that he seemed to find very droll. After about an hour we left. Outside, Antje introduced the man to us and said he was a photographer. The two of them decided to go on to some other place together. Sonia said she was tired, and I didn't feel like going along either. I wondered if Antje hadn't hooked up with the photographer so as to leave us alone in the apartment, at any rate it wasn't until much later that I heard her come home.

I kissed Sonia on the stairs, and then we kissed in the hallway. She was a bit drunk, and kept bursting out laughing while I was kissing her, also her hands were busy, now clasping behind my neck, my shoulders, my back, running through my hair. Probably we were more nervous than stimulated. I couldn't manage to undo Sonia's belt. She giggled nervously and said she had to go to the bathroom quickly. She turned the key in the lock, and I heard the toilet flush, and her brushing her teeth, but when she finally came out she was still dressed. I've got to go too, I said, and disappeared.

Sonia lay in my bed, with the covers pulled up to her chin. She had hung her clothes over the back of a chair. I started to undress, then she turned out the light, and I had to cross the room in darkness, and banged my foot against the chair with her clothes on it, which fell over with a loud crash. I swore and slipped into bed. Hello, said Sonia in a silly voice, and put out her hands toward me, as though to push me away. I said I wanted to be able to look at her, and leaned across to switch on the bedside lamp, but she clasped me around the neck and began kissing me. I felt for her body. She was in her underwear. When I went to pull off her panties, she grabbed my hands and asked me if I had condoms. Aren't you on the pill?, I asked. No, she whispered. I'm sure Antje'll have some, I said, and got up, don't go away. In the darkness I stumbled over the upset chair. I didn't find any condoms, neither in the bathroom nor in Antje's bedroom. I went back to Sonia. This time I switched on the overhead light. She blinked and turned away from the light. No luck, I said, and slipped under the covers, I'll be careful, promise. Sonia said that was too risky for her, couldn't I go out to the night pharmacy and buy some. She lay there as stiffly as she had on the beach the first time I'd kissed her. I stroked her hair. Go on, she said, be quick. When I returned half an hour later with the condoms, the light was out and Sonia was asleep.

We woke early in the morning, I don't know which of us awoke first. Silently we started caressing each other, it was as though our bodies were reaching for each other, while the rest of us was still half asleep. Sonia kissed me, she shoved her tongue in my mouth, it seemed very big to me, and I got the taste of her sleep. She had pulled off her underwear and laid herself on top of me. I still remember my surprise at her weight and warmth. We moved slowly together like two sleepy desirous animals trying to become one.

We stayed in bed all morning making love, almost without a word. Once Antje knocked on the door, put her head around the corner, and asked us what our plans were, and if we meant to have breakfast any time. When we said no, she went out without a word. Later, Sonia asked me to get her a glass of water. I pulled on my shorts. In the hallway I ran into the photographer, and we said hello. It didn't feel embarrassing at all, on the contrary, I felt a kind of satisfaction. Are you getting up at last?, called Antje from the kitchen. I didn't reply, and disappeared into the guest bedroom. Sonia had gotten dressed and pulled up the blinds, and was looking out the window. I stood behind her and embraced her. She took the glass from my hand and drank it in slow sips.

Our remaining days in Marseilles were perhaps the happiest in our entire relationship. We strolled hand in hand through the city, looked at old buildings, and stopped in front of construction sites to watch the work. At noon the sun was vertical, and in the sea of light the shadows of the trees were like little islands where we took refuge. When the heat became unbearable, we went back to the apartment. Sonia sketched, and I would read or flick through Antje's collection of antique illustrated books on all sorts of subjects.

I think Antje was a tad jealous of us, anyway she passed occasional remarks about young love, and said it prevented her from working if we hung around necking all the time. She had a show coming up in the fall, and she wasn't happy with what she'd done so far this year. At night she stayed out on the balcony with a half-bottle of wine, while Sonia and I disappeared to bed. Sonia used the bathroom first and then waited for me under the sheets, and we would kiss and embrace. Then she would turn out the lights and we would make love. When I woke up in the morning, she had pulled on her pajamas, and when I hugged her, she got up and said she didn't want to waste the day in bed. I had the feeling of her withdrawing from me, perhaps our nocturnal pleasures were embarrassing. She went to the bathroom, and when she returned, she was freshly showered and dressed. I was still lying in bed, and she sat down on the bedside, and sometimes let me pull her back in, but she fought off my caresses and gave me only brief kisses, and said laughingly I was a lazybones, and would never amount to much.

Wouldn't it be nice to live here?, she asked once. Yes, I said, either to do her a kindness or because at that moment I really believed it, forgetting that I could hardly speak a word of French, and would never land a proper job in this city. I didn't think about Munich, or of the future; time seemed to stand still, as though there was only the sea and the city and the heat. When a wind picked up, I thought about Africa. I had been looking at a picture book on the Kalahari Desert, and was sitting there dreamily. I saw great expanses of veldt full of animals, herds of animals moving over the plain, quickly and aimlessly. They trotted, galloped, and grazed. They ran across the expanse, following some invisible routes, always the same routes since the year one. They reached a water hole, a pasture, they disappeared into the distance, the wind blew away their traces.

Once there was a trivial quarrel with Antje. I had left a couple of dirty cups in the sink, and she accused us of using her apartment like a hotel. She wasn't some chambermaid, with nothing better to do than tidy up after us. Sonia felt bad, though it wasn't her fault. We quickly patched things up with Antje, but the atmosphere wasn't the same. Two days later we left.

Antje didn't get up until we had had breakfast. I made her some coffee. Sonia said she was going shopping in town. Antje asked Sonia to take her along, she had to check in on the gallery and run a couple of errands besides. I asked her if she wasn't tired. No, she said roughly, and drank her coffee standing up.

Sophie wanted to watch a movie. Just this once, said Sonia, although it was really a very common occurrence. Sonia had distinct notions of how to raise a child, and even though she kept having to make compromises, she wasn't prepared to abandon her ideal line. That way, Sophie's upbringing presented itself as a sequence of exceptions. Sophie had learned how to live with that. Each of her appeals ended in "just this once." And since Sonia and I were generally overworked and felt guilty for not spending enough time with Sophie, we rarely denied her. But only once you've fed Mathilda and changed her litter, said Sonia. Why is it always me who has to do that, groaned Sophie. You wanted a cat, said Sonia, now you have to look after her.

The two women set off. I put in a DVD for Sophie and went out to the garden. The fog had lifted a little and the sun was peeping through, but the air was still chilly. We had a few vegetable beds where we grew lettuces and vegetables in summer, but this year had been so rainy that we hardly harvested anything, and had neglected the garden out of annoyance. The tomato plants had rotted away, their fruits had gone black and fell off at the slightest touch and splattered on the ground. A few tiny cabbage heads lost themselves in the rampant grass, the cucumber that I'd once trained up a wooden stake had been attacked by mildew and was dried out. I ripped everything up and tossed it in the compost bin. I wanted to hoe the beds, but the ground was frozen. Instead I started to rake up the leaves that had dropped from our neighbor's great sugar maple onto our tiny patch of lawn and onto the front yard. Once Sophie came out of the house and watched me, then she disappeared inside again. Shortly before noon, Antje and Sonia returned with bulging shopping bags. Half an hour later Sonia called me in to lunch.

84

After our meal we pulled on our coats and sat down outside to drink our coffee. Sonia talked to Antje about her
time as in intern. Antje said Marseilles had changed, even
since Sonia's latest visit. The city was much cleaner than
before, but it had gotten a bit boring too. Which is fine by
me, she said, I'm not twenty anymore. Sonia said she had
found it hard to settle in there, if Antje hadn't introduced
her to a few people, she would probably have spent the entire six months alone. You had so many visitors, said Antje.
That's not true, said Sonia, I did nothing but work all the
time. Even so, it was perhaps the time of her life. Albert
had trusted her, and she had learned an incredible amount.
Do you remember the silly fellow who visited you?, asked
Antje. The one who went on and on about udders? Jakob?,
I asked. He didn't visit me, Sonia said, he just turned up
one day. Anyway, he came and stayed with us, said Antje.
You thought he was so frightful, didn't you?, I said. He just
wrote to me a couple of times, said Sonia. He got the address from my parents. He called them and said he was an
old friend, and they had no reason not to believe him.

Jakob had written Sonia long, wild letters that she didn't
answer. Then, in spring, shortly before she was due to return to Munich, he had gone to Marseilles and rung Antje's
doorbell.

And I let him in, said Antje. How was I to know that
he and Sonia hardly knew each other? When she got back
that evening, she was in for a shock. Why didn't you just

85

throw him out?, I asked. He was all right, said Antje. And he cooked for us too.

Jakob had come with veal sausages from his village butcher, and pretzels and beer, a whole little barrel from a local brewery. Sonia laughed, Antje had asked a few friends over, and they celebrated a proper *bierfest*, bang in the middle of Marseilles. We taught the French German songs, said Antje. "Annchen von Tharau." Remember that? She started to hum the melody, and Sonia recited the words.

Würdest du gleich einmal von mir getrennt,
Lebtest, da wo man die Sonne kaum kennt;
Ich will dir folgen durch Wälder, durch Meer,
Eisen und Kerker und feindliches Heer.*

German chansons, said Antje laughing. After that we clearly couldn't throw him out anymore.

Jakob stayed a whole week with the two women. He cooked for them every night and entertained them with his strange stories. How we used to laugh, said Antje. His village must be populated entirely by idiots. He wasn't always like that, said Sonia. He seriously tried to convert me to

---

* If you were ever sundered from me / and lived somewhere that's always winter / I will go through forests and seas for you / and brave prisons and chains and enemy armies.

Catholicism. We sat up whole nights arguing. You never told me about that, I said. You don't tell me everything either, said Sonia. Antje shot me a dark look. No one spoke. Then Sonia told us about how one night Jakob declared his love for her. Seriously?, I said, and had to laugh. It wasn't funny at all, said Sonia. He cried when I told him I was going to marry you. But he took it like an absolute gentleman. To this day, he sends me a card every birthday. And we exchange the occasional e-mail. Jakob was still living on his own, she said. He was a vet, and lived in his parents' house in the Bayerischer Wald. When we were going through our rough patch, she had often called him on the phone, and he had been very helpful. He urged me to stay with you, she said. For Sophie's sake. He respects the institution of marriage and family. I wanted to say something, but when I caught the look in Sonia's eye, I just said, I'm going for a walk.

I walked through the village down to the lake. On the grounds of the Academy, I sat down on the shore. I sat in the shadow of a tree and looked out onto the water. A steamer went by, it had to be a charter tour, because the regular passenger steamers had stopped a month ago for the winter. There was no one to be seen on deck, but I could make out some shadowy shapes behind the tinted windows.

Sonia and I had chartered a boat when we got married. Her father paid for everything. There must have been eighty guests, loads of family on Sonia's side, and friends and people who stood in some relation to her and her parents. I would have been quite happy if things had been more modest, but Sonia said her parents would be disappointed if we didn't have a proper celebration. We almost argued when I said, whose wedding was this anyway? Sonia had spoken against me. A wedding was a social occasion, she said. And that's what it was. If I hadn't happened to be the groom, I'd have enjoyed it, I think. Everything was perfectly organized, the food was excellent, and the speeches were funny and suited the occasion. Only my father's speech was a bit embarrassing. He wasn't used to public speaking, and he was inhibited. In spite of that, he still seemed to feel it his duty to say something. He hadn't prepared anything and lost his way. When I saw the smug, sympathetic looks on the faces of Sonia's family, I hated her for a moment. Then my father managed to finish, and there was warm applause. Sonia hugged him, and her mother, evidently moved, went over and toasted with him. I had too much to drink that evening, and when Sonia and I were finally able to get away and disappeared into our hotel room, we were both so tired we collapsed into bed. Even so, I was unable to sleep for a long time. I could hear people talking and laughing outside long into the night, and felt slightly sorry for myself. I lay there in that grotesque four-poster bed with canopy and heart-shaped pillows, and could think of nothing but how much I was missing my friends.

A few bigger waves slapped against the shore, and then the lake was calm again. It was a strange notion, that Jakob had made a declaration of love to Sonia a matter of weeks before our wedding. I talked to her often on the phone that spring, to discuss the wedding and the honeymoon, but she never mentioned Jakob's visit. I wondered if she had any feelings at all for him. I could remember her criticizing him after Rüdiger's New Year's party. That was the night I had proposed to her. Jakob had been unlucky and too late. Probably he loved her more than I had ever done. Maybe that's why she chose me.

We got back from Marseilles in a day as well. North of the Alps the weather was changeable. The sky was cloudy, and there were lots of showers.

Sonia dropped me off at the Olympic Village. She got out of the car with me, but when I tried to kiss her, it seemed to embarrass her. Shall we have a drink?, I asked her, but she said she was too tired, she was going straight home. When shall we see each other? I don't know, said Sonia, I've got a lot going on in the next few days. In the end we made a date for Saturday.

Sonia had left me by the subway station. I got myself a cup of coffee from the stand there. The rain had stopped.

90

The sound of the evening rush-hour traffic on the wet roads surrounded me like an invisible space. I walked to the tennis courts, where it was quieter. After the long drive, I felt like being outside, but I was tired, and all the benches were wet from the rain. My coffee had gotten cold, and I dumped the half-full cup in a bin. I was relieved to be on my own again. In my recollection, the past few days appeared more real than they had to me while I was living them. It was as though it was only just dawning on me now that Sonia and I were going out together. I felt like talking to someone, to convince myself, but I didn't know who. In the end I went to the bungalow and called my parents. I told my mother about the trip, but not about Sonia. She was only half-listening, I could hear the TV on in the background.

When I called Sonia a couple of days later, to fix a time and place, she said she had arranged to go to the cinema with Birgit, one of her roommates. They were going to see *Rain Man*. I said I thought we had a date. Would it bother you if she came along?, said Sonia.

After the film, we had a glass of wine in a bar, and argued about Dustin Hoffman, whom I'd never liked, and who the girls thought was amazing. We didn't agree about the film either. I said I couldn't understand how Sonia could fall for such kitsch. She was hurt. She had treated me like a stranger the whole evening, and our difference of opinion didn't help things. When I tried to kiss her, she turned her head away, and when I tried to take her hand she withdrew it. Fairly early on, she said she had to go to bed, she was tired. I walked the two of them home. I had hoped to spend the night at Sonia's, but she said good night outside the door so emphatically, I didn't want to say anything. I'll give you a call, she said.

A couple of days later, she visited me. The weather had picked up, and we ate in the beer garden of the Olympic Village, and after that we walked in the park. For a long time we sat by the lake and discussed the competition entry Sonia was working on. She'd stopped asking me if I wanted to participate, and that was fine by me. The project didn't interest me, Sonia's ideas were all too practical for me; I didn't listen to her, and watched the girls jogging by alone or in little groups, and thought about other stuff. When Sonia paused, I cut in to ask her if we were actually an item still or not. Of course we are, she said in astonishment. I said I thought she had treated me like a stranger on Saturday. She said she was tired. Anyway, her roommates didn't know about us yet. Are you ashamed of me? Oh nonsense, said Sonia, and shook her head.

She went back to the bungalow with me that evening, and we slept together, but I had the sense she was doing me a favor. The bed over the steps wasn't especially solid, and it creaked so loud that Sonia finally asked if I was sure it would hold up. Do you think your neighbors are in? Never mind them, I said. I've heard them at it often enough. But the thought that someone might be listening to us bothered

Sonia so much that she stiffened and grabbed hold of me. Not so hard, she said, or we'll crash. She kissed me mechanically a couple of times, then she said she'd better go home, she had something in the morning she didn't want to be late for.

We were now seeing each other regularly. Sonia invited me back to her place, and told Birgit and Tania about us. She did it in such a weirdly formal way, it felt like I was being introduced to her parents. In spite of that, I didn't really have the feeling Sonia was my girlfriend. I would occasionally spend the night with her, but when we made love, I could feel her anxiousness. The least noise made her flinch. You know this isn't a crime, I said. You don't understand, said Sonia.

My internship started in September and Sonia's in October. After she had sent in her competition entry, we had a couple of days free and drove to Stuttgart, to look at Mies van der Rohe's Weissenhof Estate. She had been there once before, with the class, but I'd been low on funds and hadn't been able to go with them. Now Sonia showed me around like a tour guide. She talked about stereometric form and the absence of ornament as a sign of spiritual force. To my mind the buildings were superficial and uninteresting. In their naive functionalism they were somehow of no particular period. Living isn't just eating, sleeping, and reading the paper, I said. A living room is first and foremost a place of refuge. It has to offer protection from the elements, the sun, hostile people, and wild animals. Sonia laughed and said, well, I might just as well go to the nearest cave in that case.

We spent the night in a pretty basic hotel. On the staircase there was a vending machine for drinks, and we took a couple of bottles of beer up to our room. The floor in the hallway was linoleum, but the room was carpeted, with thick curtains in the windows, reeking of cigarette smoke. We sat down side by side on the bed, drinking our beer. Suddenly Sonia started laughing. I asked her what the matter was. She said this place was so awful, you had to laugh or cry. And she preferred the former. That night we made love. Sonia was much less inhibited than in Munich, perhaps the ugliness of our surroundings had a liberating effect on her. When I stood by the window later, smoking, she came up to me and took the cigarette from my hand, and had a puff. You're cute when you smoke, I said, clasping her waist. Kiss me. Once in a blue moon, she said, pressing herself against me.

Sonia insisted on paying for the room, her father had given her money when she graduated. But surely not to keep a fancy man on, I said. Do they even know about me? Sonia hesitated, and I noticed that the subject was difficult for her. I had told my parents about Sonia, albeit in a casual way, and they hadn't asked me any further questions.

Then my internship began, and now it was me who never had any time. The firm was on the edge of the city, and I rarely got back from work before nine or ten. I was so

exhausted then that I didn't feel like going out afterward.
Sonia called me every day, but it didn't seem to bother her
that we only saw each other on weekends.

At the end of the month I had to move out of my bungalow in the Olympic Village. Birgit and Tania were fine
with me staying in Sonia's room until further notice. Before I could offer Sonia my help, she had already carted
her things back to her parents' house and tidied the room.
I didn't have a lot of stuff. A tabletop on two sawhorses, a
mattress, and a couple of cardboard boxes full of books
and records. I bequeathed the rest of my stuff to the person
moving in after me. Rüdiger and Sonia helped me move,
then we went for a meal together, and then they took the
train back to Lake Starnberg. I had asked her to stay with
me, but she wanted to spend her last few days in Germany
with her parents. On the eve of her departure we met up
one more time. Sonia was nervous and eager to get home.
We said good-bye without making any promises. Be good,
was all Sonia said as she got into her car. You too, I replied,
and waved to her till she turned the corner.

We were a good match, so everyone said, but we both
knew that plenty could happen in six months. Sonia had
said she didn't want to commit herself in any way. She was
right at the beginning of her career. Maybe she'd stay in
Marseilles, or she'd accept an offer to go somewhere else.
She would love to work in a big bureau in London or New
York. We'll see, I said. Maybe it'll be good for us to be

separated for a while, Sonia said, and if we're still together come the spring, well then, so much the better.

Sonia wrote me every week, so regularly that it seemed to me to express a duty rather than a need. She wrote to say she was fine, and she asked when I could visit. I replied that I had a lot on my plate, and wouldn't be able to get away from Munich very easily. Maybe over the holidays. But she'd be in Starnberg with her parents then, she wrote. I got the sense she didn't really mind conducting a long-distance relationship. She could use it to keep other men away, and give herself wholly to her work. Her boss was a genius, she wrote. She always referred to him by his first name, as though they were old friends, and after a very short time, it was all "we" and "us." We're building a day care. We're entering a competition to build a conference center. We think architecture should appeal to all the senses, it wants to be seen, touched, smelled, and felt. I resisted the temptation to tell her to cut the crap. Presumably I was just jealous. The office where I was an intern specialized in unimaginative office buildings. The company motto was the customer knows best, or maybe money doesn't stink. In one of her letters, Sonia quoted Hermann Hesse. *So that the possible can come into being, the impossible has to be attempted again and again.* I pictured her walking along the beach with her Albert, the mistral playing in her hair, and her appealing to all the senses of her boss. She was gazing at him adoringly and he was quoting

Hermann Hesse to her. Every beginning has its magic. I felt good in my jealousy, even though I was sure that Sonia was faithful to me, and that she took our relationship seriously, maybe more seriously than I did. When we talked on the phone, occasionally we made plans, we discussed founding a firm one day, after we'd accumulated some experience. But I wasn't accumulating any experience, my work consisted principally of constructing models and filling in work schedules. For months I sat in a windowless office, sketching identical staircases. Even though I was kept busy, I was bored. Boredom had a seductive charm. Secretly I enjoyed having no responsibility and nothing to aim for. I didn't go looking for a better job, ordered no competition guidelines, and read no architectural journals. Instead I immersed myself in books by dead authors. I read Poe and Joseph von Eichendorff, Mircea Eliade and Giambattista Vico, and it was as though their writings contained a truth that I could at least sense, though it could never be proved. By way of Aldo Rossi I came across Étienne-Louis Boullée, a pre-Revolutionary French architect who designed melancholy monumental structures not one of which had been built. I became fascinated by his way with light, which in his drawings wasn't a given, but more like a substance. It looked as though the buildings were pushing back against a stream of light, against the stream of time.

I filled notebooks with confused thoughts and designs for enormous purposeless constructions, archives, cenotaphs, fortresses half sunk into the ground, almost windowless rooms that light barely penetrated.

When, quoting Aldo Rossi, I said in a letter to Sonia that every summer felt like my last, she shot back that to her, this summer had felt like her first. She had never cared for Rossi's melancholy and fixation on the past. She believed the world could be transformed by architecture, and when I objected that all the great things had already been built, she mocked me and said I was just trying to excuse my lack of ambition.

Our shared apartment was on the second floor of a tenement building on a narrow street. As long as Sonia had lived there, I had always enjoyed visiting, but since she moved out, I felt rather ill at ease in the rooms. The arrangement of space was somehow inharmonious, and it didn't get enough light. My room was long and narrow and disproportionally high. I had set up my table in front of the window, but even so, whenever I sat down to work, I felt simultaneously exposed and jammed in. The only heating in the apartment was an oil-burning stove in the living room, and when I closed my door for privacy, I noticed the room got cold very quickly. So when I was at home, I spent most of my time lying on my mattress, which was in one corner of the floor, and read or dozed.

My living with Birgit and Tania turned out to be prob-
lematic. Sonia had talked them into taking me in, but
actually neither of them wanted to share with a man. In
the case of Birgit, who was just gearing up for her thesis, I had often had the feeling before that she resented
me, but when I raised it with Sonia, she only laughed and
shook her head, and said Birgit had grown up with two
sisters, she just wasn't used to encountering a man outside
the bathroom door every morning. Tania, my other roommate, worked as a medical assistant at the hospital in Bo-
genhausen. To begin with, we had gotten along rather well,
but lately she'd gotten into discussions about drugs and
upbringing and expressed arch-conservative views that I
hadn't expected in her. She was away for weeks on end at
congresses or courses, and each time she returned, she had
a new pet theme, feminism or antiauthoritarian rearing or
homosexuality, which she would proceed to blame for the
approaching end of the world. Shortly after Sonia left, Tania
started talking obsessively about AIDS, and developed an
absurd preoccupation with hygiene. She brought back bottles of disinfectant spray and left them out in the kitchen
and bathroom, and each of us got his own individual shelf
in the fridge, and there was no more sharing of food. Then
Tania started bringing home people who were put up in the
living room, and who tried to convert Birgit and me to their
opinions. It turned out that they were all members of a

dubious anthroposophical society. Birgit would often argue with them, while I retreated to my room or demonstratively switched on the TV and turned the volume so high that it wasn't possible to conduct a conversation over it. The atmosphere in the apartment deteriorated. Even so, I was only halfhearted about looking for a new place to live.

Most of the people I knew from college had moved away. Ferdy had found a job in Berlin and Alice had gone with him, Rüdiger was touring Latin America and sending back postcards from Buenos Aires and Brasília. I envied him, not so much the trip itself as the energy to have undertaken it in the first place. I had the feeling of being the last person left in the city. That's the only way I can explain the fact that at the end of October, I started seeing Ivona again.

It was very simple. I told them in the office that I had a dentist's appointment, and went to the bookstore just before closing time. Ivona came out from the back of the store, just as on the occasion of my first visit. She stood silently behind the counter and straightened the saints' pictures and the little books compiled from nature photos and quotations from Scripture. She wore beige knickerbockers and a sort of folksy embroidered blouse. I could feel her eyes on me, but when I looked over, she looked away. I felt an incredible desire to sleep with her, in the

midst of this Christian kitsch and self-help and inspi-
rational literature. Are you on your own?, I asked. She
didn't reply. I lifted the curtain and peered into the back
room. In spite of the drawn curtains, the space was murky
this time. The window opened onto a tiny yard that probably caught the sun only for an hour or two in the middle
of the day. In the center of the room stood massive old
oak desks, and on the walls were shelves containing cardboard boxes and stacks of plastic-sealed books. There was
a smell of dust and paper, and more faintly of candle wax
and human sweat. I sat down on one of the desks. Ivona
followed me, and stopped in the entry. Come on, I said.
She said she was closing in five minutes. The bell chimed
in the shop, and Ivona disappeared. I heard her speaking, and couldn't understand a word, it must have been
Polish. I looked through a chink in the curtain and saw
a pretty blond woman roughly Ivona's age. The two of
them clasped hands, and the blond woman was laughingly trying to persuade Ivona of something, who shook
her head, and seemed to be explaining. I sat down on the
desk again, and waited. Shortly afterward, the bell went
again, and then I heard the key turn in the lock.

I had expected Ivona would complain to me about what
had transpired at our last meeting, or that I hadn't been in
touch for such a long time, but she stopped an arm's length
in front of me, and stared into space. I stood up, took a step
toward her, and embraced her. She didn't resist, just freed

herself quickly to switch off the light, and pull the curtain across.

I took off her pants and underwear, and kissed and stroked her. She moaned and turned her head from side to side. She almost looked to me as though she was faking, but I didn't care. I got undressed, and we lay on the bare floor, and Ivona started kissing and stroking me back. Only when I tried to enter her did she refuse me. When I finally turned away from her, she whispered something in Polish. I didn't ask what she was saying, I could imagine it well enough, and I didn't want to hear it. Don't go yet, she said. I've got lots of things to do, I said. Do you want something to eat?, she asked. I said I didn't have the time, and got up. Will you come again? Yes, I said, and I went.

I went back to the office to finish a couple of things. My boss had already left. At eight I called Sonia. She wasn't home. Two hours later, after I was finally finished with my work, I tried again. This time, Sonia picked up, and I asked her if she was so busy. But I wasn't jealous, and I listened patiently as she told me about some new project she was working on. Then I talked to her about my work. Sonia said she hadn't heard me in such a good mood for ages. And it was true, I was perfectly calm, and made jokes, and told her I missed her. I miss you too, said Sonia. We'll see each other at Christmas. I was astonished not to feel guilty at all—on the contrary, I felt more connected to Sonia than I had in a long time.

When I turned up in the shop the next time, Ivona asked me to go back to the student residency with her. It was one of the few times she ever asked me for anything.

From then on, I only saw her in the dorm. Her room seemed like it might belong to an old woman or a little girl. It was stuffed full of junk, faked memories of a life that hadn't happened. At the head of the bed was a small plastic crucifix, the walls were covered with postcards and framed Bible sayings. On the bed were any number of soft toys in garish colors, the kind you can buy at railway station kiosks. On the floor were piles of romance novels, Christian manuals, and Polish magazines. In amongst them were scattered clothes and tights, clipped recipes, and cheap costume jewelry. The pokiness, the untidiness, and the absence of any aesthetic value only seemed to intensify my desire. There was nothing there to inhibit me, by reminding me of my life and my world. It was as though I became someone else in that room, an object in Ivona's chaotic collection of treasured and neglected knickknacks.

I turned up whenever it suited me and whenever I could. Ivona was there every evening, she didn't seem to have anything to do but wait or hope for me to come. Usually the TV was going, and when she made to turn it off, I said no, and we undressed and kissed and embraced to the soundtrack of some schlocky film or other. Usually I was gone before the film was even over. I never spent the night there, for fear Tania or Birgit might tell Sonia about it. Anyway, I couldn't imagine waking up beside Ivona, I could only stand her company when I was aroused.

My third or fourth meeting with Ivona was the day after the Wall came down. I had sat up half the night in front of the television and was tired when I went to her place the next evening. I asked her what she thought about it all. She shrugged her shoulders. I said I wasn't sure I agreed with reunification, and totted up the pluses and minuses as though the future of Germany were somehow mine to give. Ivona listened to me hold forth with an apathetic expression, as though it was all no concern of hers. She seemed to live in her own little world, not registering what was going on around her.

I noticed that Ivona took steps to make herself prettier. She started to apply makeup and did her hair, and took trouble with her clothes. When I said I didn't like her dolling herself up, she stopped. She seemed to take it as proof of love that I noticed her appearance and bothered to comment on it. Sometimes she showed me two outfits and asked me, which do you like best? I pointed to one of them, even though I was completely indifferent, and then she disappeared behind the closet door to put it on, and I followed her to watch and pulled her back to bed, still in her underwear. When she went to the toilet too, I sometimes followed her, her sense of shame provoked me until she had completely lost it and accepted everything I did, and did everything I demanded of her. With one sole exception.

When I stayed longer, Ivona would start to talk. She had an inexhaustible supply of abstruse stories, featuring the Black Virgin of Czestochowa or some other sacred figure performing miracles in the lives of ordinary people. It would start with a lost bunch of keys, and end up with a miracle cure or a surprise late pregnancy. She talked hastily and not looking at me, it was as though she was talking to herself, an endless litany. At those moments, I got a glimpse of what a terribly lonely person she was. Sometimes she would talk about her Pope, whom she revered, and who was something approaching a saint in her eyes. When I criticized him, she wouldn't say anything, and when I'd said my piece, she would resume where she'd left off. My words seemed not to have reached her.

Our encounters always followed the same pattern, rarely lasting for longer than an hour and sometimes a lot less. Ivona wasn't a sophisticated lover, she had no experience and no imagination. When she touched me she was either too hesitant or too rough, when I touched her she barely reacted, or faked a reaction. The thing that kept me fascinated with her was her utter devotion. Her unconditional love for me, however purely random, drew me irresistibly to her and, by the same token, repulsed me the instant I was satisfied. Then I would feel the need to hurt her, as though that was my only way of breaking free.

Do you think your Holy Father would approve of what you're doing?, I asked her one time, do you not think it's a sin even if we don't technically make love? I accused her of bigotry. She didn't understand the word, I had to explain it to her.

I don't know how I can excuse my behavior, I can't remember how I justified it to myself at the time. All I know is that I got to be more and more dependent on Ivona, and that while I continued to think I had power over her, her power over me became ever greater. She never demanded anything from me, was never hurt when I stayed away for days on end because I was busy in the office or didn't feel like visiting her. Sometimes I'd tell Ivona about other women to get her upset, but she took it, and listened, expressionless, while I raved about the beauty, the wit, and the intelligence of other women. Perhaps she didn't know she had power over me. Perhaps she mistook my submissiveness for love.

The situation in the apartment had deteriorated to the point where we only communicated by means of little notes that we stuck on the fridge door. Tania had come up with a roster of household duties, which Birgit and I strenuously ignored. The whole apartment reeked of disinfectant, and it was often cold, because Tania would turn down the heat to keep the germs from multiplying so quickly, as she explained. Her visitors stayed longer and longer, and began to take a hand in our business. When I returned from a weekend with my parents once, my bed had been stripped. I brought it up with Tania, and she said a friend of hers had spent the night in my room, surely I had no objection? I stood by silently while she sprayed my bed with disinfectant and put on new sheets. From that day on, I locked my door when I went out, and belatedly became serious about looking for somewhere else to live.

Finding a new place wasn't easy. I was on three thousand marks a month, which wasn't bad for an intern, but that sort of money didn't buy you much. I looked at all sorts of apartments without being able to decide. Over time, I started to take pleasure in inspecting places that were obviously hopeless. When I told the landlords that I was an architect, they treated me with respect and left me all sorts of time. A few of the apartments were still occupied, and it was fascinating to see the different ways people arranged themselves, and how much you could infer about their lives from a few objects. It was always embarrassing being taken around by tenants, peering into closets that were stuffed with junk and inspecting kitchens full of dirty, food-encrusted plates and withered herbs on the windowsill. One tenant had locked himself in the bathroom. The super took me around and knocked on the bathroom door, but the tenant didn't make any noise. He's been given his notice, said the super, and I can promise you he'll be out by the end of the year, even if it means calling the cops.

In the end I found a small three-room apartment on the top floor of an old building in Schwabing. I'd fallen in love with it on the spot. It was unrehabbed, and just had an old oil-fired stove, but the layout was good, and the rooms were light and had the sort of attention to detail that you don't often find in newly built homes. I told Birgit about it that same evening. She wasn't too thrilled about the prospect of having to deal with Tania and her loopy friends on her own. She said if she could afford it, she would move out tomorrow.

The holidays came nearer. Lots of my friends were going to spend Christmas with their families, and had announced their visits. Ferdy and Alice were coming, Rüdiger wrote from São Paulo, the last stop on his South American tour, even Jakob the vet called. He had accepted a job as an assistant in Stuttgart, and said he would be in Munich briefly on his way to the Bayerischer Wald, and did I feel like going out for a beer with him. Sonia would be the last to return, she still had lots of work to finish, and booked her flight for the morning of the twenty-fourth.

I made a date with Jakob. Before I saw him, I went to Ivona's. As we sat on the bed and got dressed, on some whim I asked her if she felt like going out and having a beer with me. I don't know what got into me. It was risky, I had to consider the possibility of Jakob running into Sonia on one of the days after Christmas. Perhaps it was a similar impulse to the one that prompts people to show off their scars, some absurd pride in damage.

Not since that first evening had I gone anywhere in public with Ivona. The notion of being seen together by one of my acquaintances was at once terrifying and beguiling. Whether I walked fast or slow, Ivona always trailed a couple of paces behind me. On the bus, she didn't sit down, but stood in front of me at my seat. When we reached our stop, I got out without a word and just glanced back quickly to see if she was following me.

I had arranged to meet Jakob in a bar we would never have gone to as students, one of those soulless beer halls in the inner city, beloved of tourists. Ivona sat on the bench along the wall, and after a short hesitation I sat down next to her. Jakob was a quarter of an hour late. We shook hands and I introduced the two of them. Ivona's from Poland, I said. I looked Jakob in the eye but saw no reaction. He just smiled, and shook hands with Ivona. Then he started talking about his dissertation, which was something about morbid changes to cow udders. It was bizarre watching this peasanty guy drinking beer and simultaneously holding forth about some complex diagnostic procedures that I was a long way from understanding. He asked me about my work. I kept my answers short. Then he asked Ivona what it was she did, and she said she worked in a bookstore. He asked where in Poland she came from, and why she had come to Germany, and whether she intended to go home ever, now that the East was opening up. Ivona said she didn't know. I was waiting the whole time for Jakob to make some remark, or give me some look, but he talked to Ivona as though it was the most natural thing in the world. He even tried out a couple of Polish phrases he had picked up on his parents' farm from migrant agricultural workers: left and right, and watch out, and postage stamp.

What was strange was that I felt a kind of jealousy when I heard the two of them talking together so easily. It wasn't that I was scared of Jakob taking Ivona away from me, but I sensed a sort of harmonious understanding between them that I couldn't account for. Jakob wasn't even especially attentive toward Ivona, he just treated her normally. She seemed to blossom in his company, whereas she was clumsy and inhibited when she was with me. I started to stroke the inside of her thigh under the table. She moved slightly away from me, but I didn't stop, and did little to hide what I was doing from Jakob. It was childish, but I couldn't stop till Jakob finally got up and smilingly said he didn't want to impose on us anymore.

When we said good-bye outside, he asked if I had any news of Sonia, the blonde who had studied with me. Immediately I understood that she was the reason why he wanted to see me. She's in Marseilles, I said. Are you in touch with her still? Sure, I said, and nodded. I looked at Ivona as I said it, but she had turned aside and was facing the other way. Maybe he'd be back after Christmas, he said, when he was with his parents he got a little stir-crazy at times. How about the four of us doing something together? I said he had my number, he could give me a call when he was next in the city.

A few days later I met Ferdy and Alice for lunch. Alice was pregnant, and they were getting married in the spring. Ferdy said he wanted to start his own architectural firm, he was going to try his luck in the East, there would be a lot of work there, it promised to be a sort of El Dorado for architects. He had made a couple of important acquaintances. Alice fussed when he lit a cigarette, and he meekly put it out. He had gotten fatter, and when he ordered pig's trotters, she said he shouldn't eat such heavy things, and pinched him in the gut. She kept on at him the whole time. It didn't seem to bother him at all, on the contrary, he seemed extraordinarily pleased with himself, as if all this was exactly what he'd always wanted. Alice asked me if I was going to Rüdiger's New Year's party. Rüdiger had asked Sonia and me, but I didn't want to accept until I talked with her. I said yes, we would probably go.

When Alice went off to powder her nose, Ferdy asked after Ivona. He had talked to Jakob on the phone, who had told him about seeing me and her together. He grinned unpleasantly. He'd never thought I was the type. But why in God's name didn't I get myself a better-looking lover while

I was at it? Who says she's my lover? Ferdy laughed. He couldn't imagine what else Ivona could be good for. And frankly, he didn't think she'd be particularly good for that either. But maybe she had hidden talents? Alice came back from the ladies' room and said she was feeling sick and wanted to leave, and the two of them headed out.

That evening I went to Ivona's. I told her to take her clothes off, and I sat and watched her. When she was completely naked, she lay down on the bed, like a patient on a doctor's table. I stood by the bedside and looked down at her, and asked her when she was going back to Poland. She tried to cover herself up, but I pulled the blanket away. She wasn't going back, she said, and she looked at me as though she expected me to be overjoyed about it. I can't see you anymore, I said, I've got a girlfriend. Since when? I told her I'd been with Sonia since the summer. Before me? Shortly after actually, I said. That seemed to please her, for the first time I caught a sort of flash in her eyes that seemed to say, I was first, I'm in the right. But she didn't say anything. We don't belong together, I said, reasoning with her, surely you must see that. You have different interests, you come from a different country, another world, really. That might not seem to matter to you, but in the long run those are the things that matter in a relationship. You wouldn't get along with my friends. What would you talk to them about? Do you understand? Ivona was stubbornly silent the whole time. When I was done, she said in a quiet, firm voice: I love you. Well, I don't love you, I said.

Before I left, Ivona had pushed a parcel into my hands, wrapped in gift paper. I didn't unpack it until I got home. It was a knitted sweater with a hideous geometrical pattern.

A few days later my new landlord called me. He had had the walls painted, he said, and I could move in any time. Ferdy helped me with my things, and went to IKEA with me, where I picked up a bed, a bookshelf, a rag rug, and a so-called starter set for the kitchen. We spent the evening assembling the furniture.

Ferdy told me about Alice. He seemed to be very enthusiastic about life as a couple. The hunt is over. I laughed. You of all people. Student life had never been his thing, he said, even if he had enjoyed it. He always longed to settle down somewhere, earn money, get some stability. It didn't mean stumbling blindly through life.

Isn't this fun, he said, holding up two pieces of wood that seemed to fit together. Yes, as long as you've got a screw, but there's always a screw missing in these things. Ferdy said that was a matter of attitude, and he kept on working. When the bed was finally done, he said, you see, there's no screw missing at all.

Furnishing the apartment was enjoyable, and gave me something to do to distract me from my introspection. I

113

found an old cherrywood table in a junk shop, and four chairs with straw seats and backrests. I hung up some lamps, put a few posters on the walls, and moved my books onto the shelves. The day before Sonia's arrival, the place looked really cozy. There were flowers on the table and the fridge was stocked. I'd even screwed in a nameplate.

Up until now I'd always taken care to own as little stuff as possible, so as to be mobile and unencumbered, but the more I bought, the more pleasure I took in my possessions. I walked through my apartment and ran my hands over the new things, picked up all the unused items and turned them over in my hands as if they promised me a different life. I switched the lamps on and off, pulled books down from the shelf, and put an LP on. In the bedroom was the sweater that Ivona had given me. I tried it on. The fit was perfect, but the pattern hurt to look at. I wondered whether I should throw it away on the spot, but I couldn't decide, and draped it over a chair in the living room.

The next morning I went to the airport to pick up Sonia. It was almost three months since the last time we'd seen each other. I was there before the plane landed, and had to wait a long time before Sonia finally came through customs. Even though I kept a picture of her on my desk, I was still astonished to see her, as I always was every time I saw her. She had gotten her hair cut really short, and was wearing a blue-and-white-striped sailor's jersey. She was tanned, and with her supple upright posture, she stood out a mile from the ruck of other passengers. When she caught sight of me, she beamed. She put down her bags and ran up to me, then stopped not quite sure what to do, till I took her in my arms and kissed her.

On the way into the city Sonia didn't talk about anything except her work. She said she had done some sketches on the flight, and showed me her notebook. She had learned a lot in those three months, that was obvious from the confidence of the drawing, her resolute and unwavering line. Altogether Sonia struck me as having grown up. She spoke more quickly and she laughed a lot, and when the taxi stopped, she paid the driver before I even had time to get my wallet out.

She seemed to approve of the apartment. She rapped on the walls and opened the windows and flushed the toilet. Well?, I said. I'll take it, she said. We stood next to each other in the bathroom and looked at ourselves in the mirror. Two beautiful people in a beautiful apartment, said Sonia, and laughed. I turned and kissed her, and thought of the beautiful couple in the mirror kissing as well, and that excited me more than the actual kiss itself. I reached into Sonia's short hair with my hand and rubbed her shaved neck. You look like a boy. She laughed and asked if I'd gone off her? I stepped behind her and placed my hands over her breasts, and said, luckily there were still a few points of difference. When I tried to pull the sweater over her head, she turned to face me and kissed me again and said, not now. I had the

115

feeling she was blushing under her tan. Come on, she said, let's not be late, my parents are waiting.

While we'd been students, I'd been out to Sonia's a couple of times, but either her parents weren't home at the time or else they just gave us a cursory greeting. Presumably they had no recollection of me at all. I hadn't seen them since I'd started going out with Sonia, and was accordingly nervous. Sonia's mother met us at the door; she kissed Sonia on both cheeks and gave me her hand and called me by my surname. He goes by Alexander, said Sonia. Alex, I said. But she disappeared into the kitchen even as we were still taking off our coats. In the living room Sonia's father was decorating an enormous Christmas tree. Ah, there you are already, he said, shaking hands with both of us. Can I get you both a drink? He was perfectly at ease, but even so I felt a little tense. Sonia said she would take me on a tour of the house.

The house had been built in the seventies. It had rough whitewashed walls, high ceilings angled in the upstairs part, and wood paneling. The staircase was open to the living room, a very large space with ceramic floor tiles and a fireplace. Sonia showed me her old room and her sister Carla's room, who was away in America studying, and who for the first time wouldn't be home for Christmas. You'll be sleeping here, Sonia said, pointing to Carla's narrow bed. I looked at her in speechless astonishment. She lowered her eyes without saying anything and led me back downstairs.

Her parents were standing at the foot of the steps, looking expectantly up at us. Under the Christmas tree there were now a couple of presents. Sonia's father gave us all a glass of champagne, and we toasted each other. Conversation was sticky. We talked about Antje, and I wondered what use these people could possibly have for Antje's paintings. Only when Carla called long distance did the atmosphere relax a little. The three of them clustered around the phone, and each of them had a brief conversation with her. The weather in California was fine, it felt weird to be celebrating Christmas under palm trees, the Americans were incredibly hospitable. After everyone had said their Merry Christmases and the call was over, we talked about America and the Americans. I was the only one not to have been to the United States, but that didn't keep me from joining in the conversation, only to have my contributions corrected by the others. I had a completely wrong sense of the States, said Sonia's father. I contradicted him, and presumably we would have had an argument if Sonia's mother hadn't changed the subject.

The evening was full of traditions, which I failed to understand. Sonia's parents weren't religious, but the course of the evening followed a rigid plan. The candles were lit on the tree, and Sonia's mother put on a record with kitschy American Christmas songs, and turned off the main light.

For a while we sat on the lounge suite, gazing at the tree. Then the lights came on again, and the presents were unwrapped. Sonia carried on like a little girl, which bugged me. Her parents had bought me a horrible espresso machine from Alessi. For the new apartment, said Sonia's mother—the design is by Aldo Rossi. Sonia told us you're a great admirer of his work. Sonia handed me a very light box. This is from me, she said, and she watched me unwrap it. It was a cardboard model of a single-family house, very carefully done. In front of the house stood two little human figures, a man and a woman. Someday, said Sonia. I wanted to kiss her on the mouth, but she turned her head away, and I kissed her on the cheek. Here are the plans. She passed me a black-bound book of sketches and rough designs for the house. You'll have to do a lot of work to afford something like that, said Sonia's father.

Soon after dinner was over, Sonia said she was tired and was going to bed. When I stood up too, she said I could stay if I liked. It probably took two hours before I finally broke free of Sonia's father. He had an unpleasantly instructional way about him, and imparted his completely unoriginal views as if they were pieces of extraordinary wisdom. Even when we talked about architecture, he didn't hesitate to correct me. In the middle of one of his lectures, I got up and said I was going to bed. I walked up the stairs. I hesitated outside the bedroom doors. Sonia's father had followed me up the stairs and motioned to Carla's door with a frosty smile.

PETER STAMM

On the morning of Christmas Day we drove out to my parents' in Garching. There was another round of gift giving and another big meal. I hadn't seen my parents in a long time and expected they would ask me lots of questions, but they just talked about the neighbors, and the recent autumn holidays, and the garden, it was the same topics of conversation as for twenty years.

We got back late to my apartment and went straight to bed. When I kissed Sonia, she said she needed to get used to me first. There's no hurry, I said, and turned over.

For the next few days it was very cold, but the sun shone. We wrapped up warm and strolled through the city, and met people and sat in cafés. Sonia had let all her friends know she was back for the holidays, and I had to listen to the same stories half a dozen times, and drank innumerable lattes.

We met Birgit, and she told us Tania had completely lost it. Her sanitary neurosis had gotten out of control, she wore silicone gloves in the kitchen, and wouldn't touch a doorknob that she hadn't previously wiped clean. She was forever talking about Christian-humanist values, and bombarded the newspapers with letters urging a tougher stance on drugs and some anti-AIDS claptrap. We wouldn't happen to have a spare room, would we? Sonia looked at me inquiringly. No, I said, sorry. On the way home, she asked me why I'd said no. She doesn't like me. You're imagining that. Anyway, I don't feel like having roommates anymore. What do you want?, asked Sonia. Perhaps she was expecting me to ask her to move in with me when she returned from Marseilles. But I missed my opportunity, if it was one.

When we were at home, Sonia worked and I read and enjoyed the feeling of being together. Sometimes I looked in on her and remained standing in the doorway of the office, and when she asked me what the matter was, I said, nothing, I'd just wanted to see if she was still there. She smiled in bewilderment. Of course I'm still here. That's good, I said, and I went back to the living room and whatever I was reading.

At dinner I kept complaining about my job. Why don't you find another one?, said Sonia. It would do you good to go abroad for a change. I said I didn't fancy it, I didn't think it was my thing. She furrowed her brow and said she didn't know if she was coming back to Munich or not. Everything was so complicated, and the old buildings everywhere depressed her. Why don't we go somewhere where they're still building properly? Eastern Europe or America. I said my English wasn't up to it. You can learn that. If you learned French, we could move to Marseilles together. They're doing so much building, the city is really going places. I don't know, I said, and I shrugged my shoulders. Sonia didn't say anything, but for the first time since we'd been together, I had the feeling I might lose her, which made me feel relieved and afraid at the same time.

Sonia had no inhibitions wandering around the flat, but she got terribly bashful when it was bedtime. She never undressed in front of me, and when I crept into bed beside her, naked, she turned away, and talked about something or other, until I lost the desire to sleep with her. When I asked her what the matter was, she said again that she had to get used to me. Nonsense, I said. You seem to be so far away, she said. I asked what she meant by that, but she just said, hold me.

On New Year's Eve we traveled out to Possenhofen, for Rüdiger's party. When we walked from the station to his parents' house, Sonia said she'd like to live here one day, not now, but later, when she had children and her own firm. It's just a matter of finding some property on the lakefront then, I said, you've already designed the house. Sonia ignored me. And she wanted an apartment in Marseilles as well, she said. Then she would spend half the year here and the other half there. Nice plan, I said. So that the possible can come into being, the impossible has to be attempted again and again, Sonia said. It took me a moment to remember where I'd heard that before. I said that was an idiotic saying. But I have to admit, I liked the idea of living here with Sonia. I could see myself standing at a big picture window with a glass of wine in my hand, gazing down at the lake. Sonia was standing next to me in a casual pose, and we were talking about a project we were working on together. We could have a motorboat, I said. A yacht on the Med, said Sonia.

Rüdiger's mother opened the door and welcomed us warmly. She took us into the living room and vanished again. By the window Rüdiger and Jakob were talking together softly. It was exactly the same situation in which I'd just pictured myself with Sonia. Rüdiger turned and came toward us to say hello.

In the middle of the room was a big laid table, decorated with paper snakes. I read the names on the cards. Most of them were familiar enough. I'm splitting you up, said Rüdiger, you don't mind, do you? Sonia and Jakob were over by the window. I went over and threw my arm around Sonia. Jakob didn't bat an eyelid. He was telling Sonia about his dissertation in exactly the same words he'd used with me two weeks before. He asked her if she knew the Bayerischer Wald. When she shook her head, he said he would take her there one day and show her the area. The doorbell rang and Ferdy and Alice walked in, and from upstairs came a young woman I didn't know.

It was almost the same group as at the summer party, but the feeling was far starchier than it had been then. Everyone had put on good clothes and brought presents. We stood around in small groups, sipping champagne and talking terribly seriously about work and our future plans.

It seemed a little bit as though we were pretending to be grown-ups.

I talked to the woman who had come down the stairs. She was one of the very few people who weren't half of a couple. She said she was from Switzerland. I'd never have guessed, I said. From the Rhine Valley, she said, laughing, did I know where that was?

She was staying with Ferdy for the moment, she was going to apply to the Academy of Arts. She was an artist. The young woman was like a simple peasant girl, she had red cheeks and she wore a handmade sweater and wide pants with some African pattern. I asked her what sort of things she did. She shrugged her shoulders. All kinds of things, for the moment she was thinking about bread. What do you mean, thinking about bread? You know, bread, she said. What bread means. Bread, I said. Yes, she said, bread. Her father was a baker, her name was Elsbeth.

He's so awful, said Sonia in the taxi, the way he kept going on and on to me. What did he talk about?, I asked. Cow udders and folkloric costume had been Jakob's subjects of choice. He had said in all seriousness that a dirndl was the ideal outfit for the female body. And stared at her the whole night as though he had X-ray vision. It wouldn't be a bad life, you know, I said, married to a vet in the Bayerischer

Wald. Sonia made a face. You would give him eight children, and you would hold on to the cows while he injected the semen into them, and look after his ancient parents. The arrogance of it, she said, with proper indignation. He's obviously crazy about you, I said, it's not his fault. It's not mine either, she said. I always get these madmen coming on to me. If only it was someone with money for a change, or good-looking. You've got me, haven't you?, I said. She was silent for a moment, and I could tell she was thinking about a question in her head. Then she took a deep breath, made a skeptical face, and asked: Are you still seeing that Polish girl? From time to time, I said. Did she knit you that vile sweater that's in the apartment? I nodded. You'd tell me if it was anything, wouldn't you? I didn't answer right away, and then I slowly said, it was something. What do you mean? It started before we got together, I said. What started?, asked Sonia. What are you talking about?

The taxi driver didn't seem to be interested in our conversation, he had his radio on and was listening to electro music. Even so, I spoke very softly. I could easily have talked my way out of it, after all, I'd never slept with Ivona. But I didn't. I said I'd had an affair, I didn't quite understand it myself. It's finished now, I said, I ended it. Perhaps I really believed that just then, I wanted to believe it. The thing with Ivona had been really stupid, I had risked my relationship with Sonia for nothing at all. Sonia still didn't seem to understand what I was talking about. She looked at me like a stranger. I hadn't seen her cry before, and it wasn't a pretty sight. Her face seemed to melt away, her mouth was contorted, her whole posture dissolved. I tried to take her in my arms, but she slid away from me and looked out the window. She said something I didn't understand. What did you say?, I asked. Why? I don't know why. She's not good-looking, she's boring and uneducated. I have no idea.

That night we made love for the first time since Sonia's return. She had gone into the bedroom without first going to the bathroom. I went after her, and watched her get un-dressed with awkward movements. There was something broken about her, only now did it occur to me that she might have had too much to drink. She sat down on the side of the bed, her shoulders hanging down. Her hair was tousled, and when she turned toward me, I could see her eyes were shining. In bed she pressed her back against me, and I noticed that she even smelled differently than usual, perhaps because, unlike the other nights, she hadn't show-ered. Her body felt softer, more relaxed, and very warm, almost fevered. After a while, she turned toward me and held me tightly and started kissing me, very quickly and frenziedly, all over my face.

Late that night, we were lying exhaustedly side by side, not touching. I asked Sonia to marry me. Yes, she said, ten-derly, and without any great surprise or excitement. Let's talk about it tomorrow.

If we hadn't slept together that night, I probably wouldn't have asked Sonia to marry me, and she would have left just as uncertain and undecided as she'd been when she arrived. Perhaps then she would have stayed in Marseilles, or gone to England or America. I sometimes wondered afterward what would have happened to us if we hadn't gotten married, but Sonia never seemed to quarrel with destiny, not even at the worst of times, when everything seemed about to go up in smoke. She had made her decision that night, or maybe even earlier, and she stuck to it and accepted the consequences.

I got up and walked along the lakefront. I asked myself if Antje was right when she said passion was an inferior form of love. It wasn't for nothing that it didn't last. What connected me and Sonia was more than a brief intoxication. We had after all stayed together for eighteen years. Maybe our relationship worked precisely because we'd never gotten really close. Even so, I wasn't sure if I wouldn't one day find myself in a situation where I'd be willing once more to risk everything for nothing.

I went home. Sonia and Antje were still sitting on the terrace, talking. Sonia said they were going to go to the movies, they wanted to see *The Lives of Others*. We've seen that already. Yes, but Antje hasn't, said Sonia. You'll have to stay here anyway and watch Sophie. I didn't understand what Sonia thought was so great about the film. When we went to see it, she cried. The last time she'd done that was for *Schindler's List*, and I couldn't understand that either.

I sat down at the table with the two women, even though I could sense I was intruding. Are you still talking about old times? It's an inexhaustible subject, said Antje. Sonia was just telling me how her family reacted when she brought you back to meet them for the very first time. That was on Christmas Eve of '89, I said. I remember because we argued about the fall of the Berlin Wall. I expect you were against it, said Antje. I wasn't against it, I said, what I was against was prompt reunification. I think most of us at the time hoped that something of the GDR would be preserved, and that the West would be changed in some respect as well. Then Sonia's father trotted out his war experiences. That wasn't it at all, said Sonia, he was just a kid in the war. And then her parents asked me all kinds of questions about my family, I said. I was surprised they didn't ask how much my old man made. Rüdiger would have suited them better. Antje laughed. That's what Sonia just said too. They thought you were a bit rude, said Sonia, and my father had the feeling you were a socialist. He still does, I said. In Bavaria, it doesn't take much to be thought of as a socialist. I think I just wasn't good enough for them, they would rather their daughter married someone from their own circle.

Alex had to sleep in my sister's room, Sonia laughed. And you slipped in to be with him?, Antje asked. Did I?, asked Sonia. No, I said. To this day you behave like a little girl when you're with your parents. Sonia protested. Probably she was just too tired. Antje said she could remember Sonia arriving back in Marseilles after Christmas, and telling her she was going to get married. I looked at Sonia. She creased her brow thoughtfully. It's a long time ago, she said, and stood up with a sigh. I'm getting chilly out here.

Sonia and Antje left at six, they wanted to get something to eat before the film. I stuck a frozen pizza in the oven for Sophie. When we began to eat, Mathilda meowed plaintively next to my chair. She hopped onto my lap. I grabbed hold of her and dropped her on the floor again. Didn't you feed her?, I asked. Sophie made no reply. Did you hear me? Sophie looked at me furiously, and said Mathilda isn't getting anything to eat today, she pooped on my bed, and that's her punishment. I tried to explain to Sophie that you couldn't treat a cat like a human being, but she acted deaf. I lost my temper, and said if she didn't give Mathilda something to eat right away, she wouldn't get anything either. I took her plate away from her, and she got up seething with rage and ran upstairs. I ate, still furious at Sophie's behavior. Then I gave the cat some food and went up to see Sophie, but she didn't respond to my knock, and I didn't feel like giving in. When I looked in on her an hour later, she was lying on her bed, fully dressed and asleep.

I went up to the attic to look for the model that Sonia had given me back then, the house she had created for the two of us. I was pretty sure it was in one of the boxes of my student stuff, but it took me a long time to find it. It was in a shoebox, along with the plans for it. It was much smaller than I'd remembered it. The cardboard was yellowed, and the glue had come off in one or two places, the two figures that represented Sonia and me had fallen off. I found them at the bottom of the box. They were plastic figurines of the sort you can get in any model shop. I looked at the plans and sketches. Le Corbusier's influence could clearly be seen. The house occupied a relatively small area, but it was three stories and had a roof terrace. The rooms were generously cut. Light came in through a wall of windows, and through skylights on the top floor. I imagined what it would be like to live in that house, asked myself how it would have changed our lives. The house we were in now was much cozier, but there was something small-scale about it, with its narrow staircase and saddle roof. It was conventional in every way, and emanated a modesty and unobtrusiveness that might have suited me but that certainly didn't express Sonia's nature. It's absurd, she said to me once, we think about beautiful buildings all day long, but we'll never be able to afford one for ourselves. And the people we build for have no appreciation of quality. I took the model downstairs to the living room and put it on the sideboard.

Sonia and Antje weren't back until almost midnight. Antje wasn't wild about the film, but Sonia had cried again. I made myself some tea, the two women drank wine. Presumably they had had something to drink in the city, at any rate they both talked fast and volubly, and I could hardly get a word in edgewise. They talked about the film, but I got the impression the real subject was something else. Antje was aggressive, while Sonia defended herself to the best of her ability. She seemed unhappy, something was bothering her. After a while she got up and said she was going to bed. On the way to the door she noticed the model. She picked it up and turned to face us, as if to speak. For a moment she stood there with half-open mouth, and then she clumsily set the model down and quickly left the room.

Antje had settled herself comfortably on the couch. She leaned back and looked at me expressionlessly. Why should I give a damn?, she finally said. I asked her what she was talking about, and she gestured dismissively. If I hadn't brought you together, you would have found some other way. What you made of it is your affair. You're free individuals.

I wondered what Sonia had told her, what they had discussed. Strange as it may seem, I said, the only one of us not to have compromised at all is Ivona. She's the only one who knew what she wanted from the get-go, and who followed her path to the end. Didn't exactly make her happy, did it?, said Antje. Who can tell?, I said. You didn't get to the end of the story, she said. I don't know if I can tell you the end of the story, I said, but I can at least tell you how it goes on. Antje poured herself some more wine and looked expectantly at me.

I told her how I had started seeing Ivona again during Sonia's internship. I know about that, Antje said, Sonia told me. I was lonely, I said, all my friends had left the city, the office I was working in was staffed by idiots, and I was living with these two crazy women. I think the worst thing for Sonia was that it had to be the Polish girl, Antje said, she didn't understand that. She still doesn't understand it. She loved me, I said, she loves me to this day. It was as though that absolved me of all questions. You told me in Marseilles that I mustn't demand too much from Sonia. I could ask for everything from Ivona. The more I asked of her, the more she loved me. Then why did you ask Sonia to marry you?, asked Antje. I don't know, I said, maybe I couldn't stand the responsibility. Antje groaned aloud. After I split up with Ivona, I didn't hear from her for years, I said, and I couldn't say I missed her. They were difficult years. We opened our firm and took every job we were offered, renovations, little things that brought in neither money nor fame. At the same time we entered loads of competitions, were up against two hundred other firms. We worked for eighty hours a week, basically we did nothing but work. But it wasn't a bad time, for all that. We knew what we wanted. We were still living in the three-room apartment in Schwabing, we had one of the rooms equipped as an office. Sometimes we didn't go outside for days on end. I slept badly, and often I was half dead with exhaustion. Sonia's parents offered to support us, but we didn't want that. Then we won a contest to build a school in Chemnitz. Our project got some attention, and soon we got more contracts. We were able to start employing people, and move into bigger premises. Sonia was the creative brains of the enterprise. She did most of the designs, while I took on the organizational and managerial tasks. I hardly gave Ivona a thought. I assumed she was back in Poland, when one day I got a letter from her.

The letter came at the worst possible moment. I had a thousand things on my mind, a building that was supposed to be finished and was going wrong in every way, a builder who kept calling me about some guarantee or other, a contest jury that I needed to prepare myself for. Sonia had been home all that week, she had a migraine and was bedridden, and only got up for a short time in the evenings when I came home, and we had something to eat together, and then she went back to bed.

The mail had been on my desk since lunchtime, but I only got around to looking at it in the evening. The envelope was made out by hand in a clumsy writing that I couldn't recognize; there was no return address. I pulled out two pieces of paper, saw the signature, Ivona, and immediately had a bad feeling. The secretary had already left for the day, so I went to the kitchen to get a coffee. Then I sat down at my desk and began to read.

Dear Alexander, perhaps you still remember me. After everything that had happened between us, I thought it was absurd, Ivona addressing me formally. Of course I remembered her. I sometimes used to wonder what had become of her, but never made any effort to find out. She wrote to say she thought about me every day, and the lovely time we had together. She had often meant to write to me, to ask to see me again, but then she had learned that I was married now, and she didn't want to interfere. She was sure I had lots to do, she sometimes saw my name in the papers, and was proud of knowing me.

For a brief moment I had the absurd thought that Ivona wanted to blackmail me, but she had nothing on me. Sonia knew about our affair, and after that night when I told her about it, I hadn't seen Ivona again, I just stopped going, and she'd never tried to get in touch. Sure, I'd behaved badly toward her, but that wasn't a crime.

The reason she was writing, I read on, was that she was in dire straits. She was still illegally in Germany, getting by on badly paid jobs off the books, cleaning and child minding and occasional little bits of translation work for a Christian publisher in Poland. The money had always been enough, Ivona wrote, she had even been able to support her parents on it, who had had a hard time after the collapse of Communism in Eastern Europe, but a few months ago, she had gotten sick, some abdominal condition. She never had health insurance, she had just been lucky enough to stay well. Now she was facing expenses that dwarfed her income. She had turned to God for advice, and one night in her dreams she had seen me as her rescuer. Even then she had hesitated for a long time before asking me for help. If I wasn't able to give her anything, she wouldn't bother me anymore. I owed her nothing, she would see any help as a charitable act, and try to pay me back as soon as possible.

The letter was cumbersomely expressed. I was pretty sure someone must have helped Ivona write it. Even so, the formulations were full of that blend of submissiveness and impertinence that had struck me about her from the start. I could picture her face before me, the expression of humility that made me wild with lust and rage. Ivona had signed with first and last names. Below her signature was an address in Perlach and a phone number. I pocketed the letter, shut down the computer, and went home.

The lakeside house of Sonia's dreams turned out to be beyond our means. Instead we lived in a row house in Tutzing, away from the lake. We had been able to buy the house after an aunt of Sonia's had died and left her a small inheritance. The first time we looked at it, we wandered into a small room under the eaves with a slanting ceiling and Sonia said, this is the nursery. I didn't say anything, and we talked about a couple of modifications. But that same evening, Sonia brought up the subject again. She said she didn't have that much time left in which to get pregnant, after thirty-five things got critical. We had a very objective conversation about the pros and cons of having children of our own, and in the end decided that Sonia would come off the pill.

After some years at the planning stage, the building work finally began on the school in Chemnitz. I rented a room there, and often stayed away all week. It was only on Sonia's fertile days that I absolutely had to be in Munich.

In spite of, or maybe even because of her beauty, Sonia was pretty inhibited. She was incapable of passion, and I sometimes got the feeling she was watching herself while we made love, to make sure she kept her dignity. Initially, synchronizing our nights to her ovulation had a positive effect on our sex life. On those evenings Sonia was nervous, she blushed easily and upset glasses and knocked things over. Then she would disappear into the bathroom for a long time, and when she came out and joined me on the sofa in her silk wrap, it felt as though she was offering herself to me, which was a thought that stimulated me. Sometimes we made love on the couch, and I thought Sonia was turned on as well, and forgot herself at least for a little while. But when she didn't get pregnant, my feeling of failure got more pronounced, and I lost all pleasure in this game.

Birgit, who had been Sonia's roommate in their student days, had opened her own practice by now. She was Sonia's gynecologist, and ran all kinds of tests, and sent us to specialists. Finally she told us that medically everything was okay, and she urged Sonia to work less, but we couldn't afford to take advice like that. It'll be all right, said Birgit. Don't think about it so much, then it'll just happen naturally.

After the appointment, the three of us went for a drink together. Conversation turned to Tania. She and Birgit had continued to live in the apartment together for two years after I moved out. Tania's hygiene neurosis had gradually abated, but she'd gotten crazier in other ways. She subscribed to German nationalist papers, Birgit told us, and expressed extreme right-wing views. I couldn't invite anyone back to the apartment anymore, I would have been ashamed if they'd seen who I was living with. Also, Tania had grown increasingly suspicious. She had developed a thoroughgoing paranoia. She ended up marrying a Swiss guy who was also a member of the organization she had joined, and she had gone to live with him in Switzerland.

But it was so nice at the beginning, said Sonia, do you remember? How we used to cook meals together? She was always a bit uptight, said Birgit. She took everything so fantastically seriously, and had theories and views about everything. She couldn't allow things just to be. Like any true believer, in other words, I said. Sonia said that was a mean thing to say. It's not the worst people who end up in sects, said Birgit. It's the seekers, the ones who are missing something, and can't live without it anymore. Then they go and hang their hearts on some guru or some idea that's in the air just at that time. Something that gives them security. A relationship can give you just as much security, said Sonia. Money gives you security, said Birgit. I said I hoped to be able to endure insecurity. Birgit laughed. If you expect a certain standard of living, there's only the appearance of freedom for you anyway. Who said that?, I asked. Birgit shrugged her shoulders. Me? No idea. The only alternative is sainthood.

The office did better than we could have dreamed, we had taken on more staff, but somehow there wasn't any less work for the two of us to do. You can't plan everything, said Birgit. We've got time, said Sonia, and if it's not meant to be, then it's not to be. I knew how much she wanted a baby, and I felt bad that I couldn't make it happen for her. We stopped talking about it, only sometimes Sonia would say she was fertile just then, and I would feel sorry for her, which didn't make me perform any better. When we moved into the house, we used the room under the eaves as a storage room, but Sonia didn't stop referring to it as the nursery.

On the day Ivona's letter arrived I happened not to have my car with me. I had belatedly taken it to the mechanic that morning to have summer tires put on, and had gone to work by subway. It was a fine day, and after work I went to the station on foot, and was thinking about Ivona. The thought that she was still living in Munich was somehow disagreeable to me. I hadn't seen her for almost seven years. It was surprising that we'd never bumped into each other in all that time, on the street or on a bus or in a store. I was sure I would recognize her instantly if I did happen to see her. Perhaps she was observing me, the way she did back then in the beer garden. I stopped with a jolt and spun around. A man who was following hard on my heels brushed past me and muttered, asshole. Not a trace of Ivona.

It had been my intention to tell Sonia about the letter and ask for her advice, but when I got home I saw that she still had her migraine, and I decided not to. She would only worry herself needlessly, or get all suspicious or something. I would call Ivona, meet her somewhere if it wasn't possible otherwise, and lend her the money, provided the amount she needed wasn't too much. And that would be an end to the matter.

Sonia said she was feeling a little better, and tomorrow she would go back to work. She had even cooked something. I'm just going to make a quick call, I said, and went to the basement where we had set up a little office.

I shut the door and rang the number in Perlach. A man's voice answered. I asked for Ivona. Just one moment, he said, and I heard sounds, a door, a hushed conversation.

Then there was silence, and I knew Ivona was on the line. I got your letter, I said. I didn't want to, said Ivona. Want to what? Ask you for help. Silence again. I'll see what I can do, I said. I'm not swimming in money. Silence from Ivona. It was no good, I'd have to see her. I asked if we could meet. The man came on the line again, said Ivona was sick, if I wanted to see her, I'd have to go there. His voice sounded dismissive, but I was pleased Ivona appeared to have someone looking after her. I asked who I was talking to. Hartmeier, he said, a friend.

The following afternoon I went to Ivona's. I told Sonia I had a meeting, and she nodded and said she'd probably stay longer at the office, a lot had accumulated in the course of her absence.

Ivona lived in an apartment building in a characterless sixties development. The buildings stood right on the road, clustered around a green space with a few trees and a neglected playground. The facade was grimy and sprayed with cryptic graffiti next to the entrance, but other than that it was in surprisingly good condition. I rang the bell and after a while a bluff-looking man with gray hair came down the stairs and opened the door for me. Hartmeier, he said, extending his hand. We were expecting you. I looked at my watch, I was only a few minutes late. He took me to the third floor, to a small, cluttered apartment. He knocked on a door and went in. I stayed in the hallway and listened to him say, with false friendliness in his voice, that he had to go. You sure you'll be all right? Then he came out and held the door open for me. When you leave, make sure she locks the door after you.

I entered the bedroom. The curtains were drawn, and it took me a moment to make out Ivona in the dimness. She was sitting on a chair beside the window. This room too was stuffed with junk. The air was stale and far too hot. I walked up to Ivona and gave her my hand. She had changed in the years of not seeing her. Her face had grown puffy, her hair was thinner. She was wearing an ugly quilted wrap of no particular color, and white socks under plastic sandals. She might be only two years older than me, but she was an old woman.

I had known her body in all its details, the heavy, pendulous breasts, the rolls of fat at her neck, her navel, the stray black hairs on her back, and her many moles. I knew how she smelled and tasted, how her body responded to touch, I knew its repertoire of familiar and less familiar movements, but when I saw Ivona sitting there, I had to acknowledge that I didn't know the least thing about her, that she was a complete stranger to me.

She told me quite freely, almost pleasurably, about her condition before the impending operation. For some time now she had had very heavy bleeding and cramping during her period. The doctor had found myomas, harmless growths in her womb, and instead of putting her on hormone treatments for years, he had suggested having the womb and ovaries removed. A perfectly routine operation, she said, the removal would be done vaginally, there was no need to open her up. It felt strange to hear the technical medical terms in her mouth. She talked about her body as though it were a malfunctioning machine. She had no fear of the operation, she said, but what made her sad was the knowledge that she would be unable to have children afterward. Thirty-eight is leaving it a bit late for babies anyhow, I thought, but didn't say anything.

Are you with someone?, I asked. Herr Hartmeier is just a friend, she said. She had the flu, that's why she was home. And he looked in on her from time to time and checked up on how she was. She asked me if I wanted some tea, and I followed her into the kitchen and watched her heat up water and take a tea bag from one of the cupboards. Her way of moving had something coquettish about it, I could think of no other word for it. Presumably, I was the only man who had seen her naked apart from her father and the gynecologist, I thought. And suddenly I had the overwhelming desire to strip her naked. I came up to her from behind, and opened her wrap, and let it fall to the ground. She was wearing a thin short nightie underneath, maybe it was the same one she had years ago. I pulled that over her head, and took off her underthings too. She turned to face me. Her features were completely expressionless.

I was pretty sure Ivona had never slept with a man, and that her panting wasn't excitement but fear. I knew I was making a mistake that could not be amended, but I was reeling with desire. I pulled her into the bedroom and onto the bed, and she lay down, and I lay on top of her. Again, I had the sense of Ivona's body having a life of its own, that when it was naked it was quite divorced from her character, and was capable of unexpected responsiveness, a mute language all its own. While Ivona kept her eyes tightly closed, and her face looked as if it were asleep, her body was awake and reacted to every touch, every glance almost, with a shaking, a trembling, tension or relaxation, in a way that both excited and repulsed me.

At five I called Sonia in the office, and explained I was running late, the meeting was taking longer than expected. Then I went back to the bedroom. Ivona lay naked on the bed, her pose had something obscene about it. I lay down on top of her and she shut her eyes again.

It was almost seven before I could tear myself away. She was in the bath, and I was sitting on a kitchen stool, feeling liberated. I could hear noises in the apartment over us, and thought about the people who lived here, the human hordes who filled the subways in the morning and sat in front of the TV at night, who sooner or later fell ill from their labor and the hopelessness of their efforts. A camp of the living and the dead, as Aldo Rossi had once described the city, where only a few symbols manage to survive. Undecipherable references to people who had once lived there. I had always been half-afraid of the faceless masses for which we put up skyscrapers. I remembered the topping-out parties when we celebrated the completion of a project with the workers. How they sat hunkered together and looked at the rest of us, the investors and builders and architects, almost with scorn. Or when I visited one of these projects years later, when I saw how the buildings had been taken over—laundry hanging out to dry on the balconies, bicycles dumped higgledy-piggledy outside the doors, little flowerbeds arranged in defiance of any understanding of landscaping—then too I didn't feel annoyance so much as fear and a kind of fascination with life swarming and seething and escaping our plans, the memories that sprouted here and merged with the buildings in some indivisible unity. Then I understood the remark that a building wasn't finished until it had been torn down or lay in ruins.

I remembered listening once to Sonia explaining to a school janitor why the bicycle racks couldn't be made any bigger. She talked about proportions and form and aesthetics. He looked at her in bafflement, and said, but the kids have got to park their bikes somewhere. Sonia had looked at me beseechingly, but I had just shrugged my shoulders, and said the janitor was right. She shook her head angrily and stalked out without another word.

Ivona emerged from the bathroom. She looked tired. I said I had to go. At the door I asked her how much the operation cost. About four thousand marks, she said. I was surprised it wasn't any more than that. I'll lend it to you, I said, you can pay me back whenever you can. I'll bring you the money. She said she was always at home during the day. At night she went out cleaning. Don't forget to lock the door now. I had to smile. She said Herr Hartmeier had her best interests at heart.

From then on I started seeing Ivona regularly again. My feelings toward her had changed from what they were seven years ago. I couldn't claim she interested me as a human being, but I had gotten used to her, and no longer felt as aggressive toward her. I drank her herbal tea even though I couldn't stand it, and I listened to her boring stories, and sometimes I told her something from my life, some office stuff that she listened to without a trace of interest or sympathy. It was still and exclusively the physical thing that tied me to her, those sluggish hours that we spent together in her overheated room, stuck to one another, crawling into each other, together and always separate. Once, I'd just gone to the bathroom, Ivona fell asleep, and I stared at her withered body and her face, by no means beautified by the relaxation of sleep, and I asked myself what I was doing here, why I couldn't leave her. But she awoke, and looked into my eyes, and like an addict I had to lay hands on her again, and grab hold of her and penetrate her.

I asked her what she had done in all those years we hadn't seen each other. She seemed not to understand the question. She had worked. And what else? Do you see girlfriends? Did you go abroad? Do you have a hobby of some kind? Sometimes she went to events organized by the Polish mission, she said, and she had a cousin who lived in Munich too, though she hardly saw her anymore. Once a year she went to Posen to visit her family.

Religion seemed to loom even larger in her life than it had seven years ago. She went to Mass regularly, and she belonged to a Bible group. That was where she had met Hartmeier. She talked about him often. He was a plumber. One of his sons was in charge of the family business now, he devoted himself entirely to the church, ever since his wife had died a couple of years ago. Once I asked Ivona if there'd been anything between them ever. We were lying on the bed side by side, she was gripping my hand, the way a child might hold its mother's. I leaned over her, and asked, is he your lover then? Own up. She looked at me with an astonished and at the same time disappointed expression, perhaps because I doubted her fidelity. Herr Hartmeier wasn't like that. Not like me? Bruno often came to see her, said Ivona, he had said he felt very close to her, but she told him she was keeping herself for someone else. It took me a while to understand whom she meant. I should have told her that I didn't want anything from her, that I would never leave Sonia for her. The very idea seemed preposterous, to give up everything for the sake of a woman with whom I had nothing but a sexual obsession. But I guessed I would never manage to persuade Ivona to give up her idée fixe, so I didn't say anything. I think she was firmly convinced that God directed our paths, and that He had plans for her and me. Let her think that if it did her some good, I didn't care. I stood by the window and looked down at the deserted playground. It had been raining for days, and big puddles had formed on the grass. There was a large birdcage on one of the balconies opposite that was covered with a patterned cloth, maybe an old curtain. I opened the window and I could hear the sound of dripping water, the sound of flowing water, and the strained buzz of a light airplane. It was late spring, but it could just as easily have been fall. I turned to Ivona and asked her if it was true that she'd had nothing to do with men for seven years. And what if I hadn't called her? Ivona didn't reply.

I always saw Ivona during the daytime. To begin with I made up meetings, but Sonia knew what I was working on, so I had to think of something else. For years I'd suffered from occasional back pain, so now I claimed I was going to do something about it. I joined a fitness club, that way I could spend an hour or two a week with Ivona, without Sonia getting suspicious.

I had brought the money for Ivona's operation to our second meeting, but I never asked her if she had gone through with it or not. She had started working again, now she was working as a cleaner in people's homes during the day. Her hours were unpredictable, and often she canceled me at the last minute, because one of her employers needed her to be there. When she told me again that she wouldn't have any time this week, I said I would pay her. She didn't reply. I'll pay you, I said, how much do you want? I had expected her to be insulted, but she just said she got paid ten marks an hour for cleaning. All right, I said, I'll give you twenty. It was a bad joke, but now every time we parted I left her some money. I'd never gone to a prostitute, the idea of spending money on sex was offensive to me. But giving money to Ivona was something different. It wasn't payment for services received. Ivona belonged to me, and my looking after her in that way was the justification of my claims of ownership. Sometimes, I don't know what got into me, I started giving her commands, and naming a price, fifty marks if you do such and such. Maybe it was a way of humiliating myself. If it offended Ivona, she never let on. She did everything, regardless of what I offered, and she took the money with an apathetic expression, and didn't bother to count it.

We were now meeting two mornings a week at regular times. Usually Ivona wouldn't have left the house yet, and was waiting for me in her wrap. She offered me herbal tea, until I gave her an espresso machine. I drank an espresso standing up. Ivona was sitting at the kitchen table, looking at me inquiringly. Then I told her what I had planned, and we went to the bedroom, or the sitting room, or the bathroom.

It was an exceptionally rainy summer, and the city felt like a hothouse under its warm humid shroud. When I lay on the bed tangled up with Ivona, a great lassitude would come over me, our sweating bodies would seem to coalesce into one many-jointed organism that moved slowly like a water plant in an invisible current. Sometimes I dropped off into a sort of half-sleep, from which Ivona would rouse me when the agreed time came around. You have to go, she'd whisper in my ear, and I got dressed and walked out into the rain, where I only slowly woke up.

I had reckoned I would get sick of Ivona sooner or later, and get rid of her, but even though the sex with her interested me less and less, and sometimes we didn't sleep together at all and just talked, I couldn't shake her off. It wasn't pleasure that tied me to her, it was a feeling I hadn't had since childhood, a mixture of freedom and protectedness. It was as though time stood still when I was with her, which was precisely what gave those moments their weight. Sonia was a project. We wanted to build a house, we wanted to have a baby, we employed people, we bought a second car. No sooner had we reached one goal than the next loomed into sight, we were never done. Ivona on the other hand seemed to have no ambitions. She had no plans, her life was simple and regular. She got up in the morning, had breakfast, went to work. If it was a good or a bad day depended on certain little things, the weather, some kind words in the bakery or in one of the houses where she cleaned, a call from a friend with whom she had a drink after work or went to the movies. When I was with her, I participated in her life for an hour, and forgot everything, the pressure of time, my ambition, the problems on the building sites. Even sex became completely different. I didn't have to make Ivona pregnant, I didn't even have to make her come. She took me without expectations and without claims.

Her hunger for a better life was fulfilled through romance novels and TV films that always ended happily. I asked myself what she felt when she shut the book or switched off the TV. I hadn't picked up a novel in years, but I still remembered the feeling of finishing a story when I was a child, late at night or on some rainy afternoon. That alertness, that sense of perceiving everything much more clearly, even the passage of time, which was so much slower than in books. I held my breath and listened, even though I knew there was nothing to hear, and that nothing had happened or would happen. I was safe in bed, and in my thoughts returned to the story that now belonged to me, that would never end, that would grow and turn into a world of its own. It was one of many worlds that I inhabited in those days, before I started building my own and losing all the others.

Basically, my relationship with Ivona had been from the start nothing other than a story, a parallel world that obeyed my will, and where I could go whenever I wanted, and could leave when I'd had enough.

Perhaps our relationship was nothing more than a story for Ivona as well. I had been struck by the way she never talked about herself. She never asked me about my life either. I could just sometimes tell from things she said that she didn't approve of my social environment, just as she seemed to despise her own surroundings. It was as though nothing counted beyond our secret meetings.

I could understand Ivona's feelings. I too was moving in a circle I didn't really belong in, only, unlike her, out of cowardice or opportunism I had managed to come to terms with it. The splendid family holidays with Sonia's parents, the visits to concerts and plays, the male gatherings where fellows smoked cigars and talked about cars and golf, they were all part of another world. Basically, I yearned for the lower-middle-class world of my childhood, with its clear rules and simple feelings. However limited it was, it still seemed more honest and genuine to me. When I was with my parents, I didn't have to playact, didn't have to try and be better than I was. Their affection was for me as a person, and not for my achievements as an architect. And then they were much more sensitive than Sonia's parents. They noticed immediately when something was wrong. Their ethical ideas might be narrow, but they understood human frailties and were prepared to forgive anything. I was sure they would like Ivona, and would accept her as one of themselves. They had never quite warmed to Sonia, even though they would never have said as much to me. Once or twice I was almost on the point of mentioning Ivona to my mother. I was certain she would understand, even if she disapproved. Presumably the reason I didn't was that I was afraid of her advice, I knew what she would say.

In the seven years I'd been married to Sonia, I'd had a couple of brief affairs, once with an office assistant and the other time with a neighbor, whose child we sometimes babysat. Sonia had been unfaithful to me once as well. We had owned up to these affairs and gotten over them, albeit perhaps scarred by them, and afterward our union felt either better or at least more stable. But I could never have told Sonia about my relationship with Ivona. It seemed to take place in a world governed by different rules. I couldn't have explained my behavior to her—I could hardly account for it to myself.

Once I asked Ivona if she wanted to go back to her homeland. She said no, she had to stay here. I didn't ask her why. But I do admit I felt relieved to hear it.

I'd been seeing Ivona for six months or so when Hartmeier called me one day. He called me in the office, at first I didn't know who it was. Only when he said we'd met at

Ivona's did the shoe drop. He asked if he could see me. I asked what it was about, but he said he'd prefer to talk about it in private. A little reluctantly, I agreed to meet him in a café near Ivona's apartment. There were never many people there, he said. It was as though he was planning a conspiracy.

It was November, and it had been raining for days. At twelve o'clock it suddenly stopped. Now it felt cold, and there was a smell of snow in the air. When I went to the café, it was already dark outside, and I could see Hartmeier through the window, sitting over an almost empty glass of beer. He was the only patron, and was chatting with the waiter.

I walked up to his table. He stood and held out his hand formally. I ordered something, and we sat down facing one another, like two chess players. Hartmeier sipped at his beer and looked at me in silence, until I asked him what this was about. Ivona, he said. He looked somehow pleased with himself, which made me suspicious. That's what I thought, I said. More silence from him. Then he said it was a delicate situation, and he didn't want to speak out of turn, but he didn't like the way I was treating Ivona. I wondered how much he knew. I had no intention of confiding in him, so, to play for time, I asked him what he meant by that. She loves you, he said, and sighed deeply. I shrugged my shoulders. With all her heart, he added. She's waited for you for seven years, the way Jacob waited for Rachel. I only vaguely remembered the story, but I remembered that at the end of seven years, Jacob had gone off with the wrong woman. Leah, Hartmeier said. And then he had to wait another seven years. I didn't understand what he was driving at. Whether she waits for you for a year or seven or fourteen, makes no difference, he said. It's like love of the Savior, it doesn't get any less over time, in fact the opposite. Ivona's feelings are a matter for her, I said. And you? I said I didn't think that was any concern of his. I might not know this, said Hartmeier, but Ivona had sacrificed a lot for me. She was acting against her faith, which forbade extramarital sex, and with a man who was married himself. Perhaps it was hard for me to grasp, but in a certain sense Ivona had sacrificed her spiritual welfare for me. She's a free human being, I said. But the Lord saw that Leah was less beloved, and he opened her womb, said Hartmeier, and then I understood why he had summoned me. He didn't speak, and it was as though I caught a glimpse of secret triumph in his face. He seemed to be waiting for me to say something. It's not easy for me to describe what I felt. I was shocked, my pulse was racing, and I felt slightly sick in my stomach. At the same time, though, I felt a great feeling of calm and a kind of relief. I would have to talk to Sonia, she wouldn't find it easy, maybe she would leave me, but just at that moment, all that seemed unimportant.

Ivona is pregnant, said Hartmeier. I know, I said, I wasn't going to allow him his little triumph. He looked at me in bewilderment. You cannot ask that she . . . He didn't go on.

I don't ask that she do anything, I said. He said it would be a sin. I don't care if it's a sin or not, I'm not asking her to abort the fetus.

Hartmeier walked me to Ivona's. Though he was shorter than me, he set such a rapid pace I could hardly keep up with him. It seemed to have gotten colder, or perhaps I was just feeling it more, because of my excitement and uncertainty. I put up my coat collar and ran after Hartmeier. He stopped outside Ivona's building and said he wouldn't accompany me any farther. He rang the doorbell, and I heard a rustle in the intercom. Hartmeier leaned down and said in his best conspiratorial tone, he's here. Immediately the door buzzed, so loud that it startled me. Hartmeier shouldered the door open, gave me his hand, and nodded to me, as though to give me courage.

Ivona was waiting for me with an almost simple smile. She looks like a bride, I thought. We sat down in the little parlor. Ivona had made tea, and poured a couple of cups. I took a quick gulp and burned my mouth. Hartmeier told me you're pregnant, I said. She nodded. I wasn't expecting that, I said. She looked at me expectantly, with an edge of panic. I said I understood that an abortion was out of the question for her, and that of course I would recognize the child, and give her what support I could. But it wouldn't be easy for her to bring up the child all by herself. Her face took on a scared expression. She must have imagined I would leave Sonia for her. There are several options, I said, of course it would be better for the child to grow up in an intact environment than with her, after all she was still an illegal alien. I would talk to my wife, after all it was my child. Ivona didn't speak, and let her tea go cold. I said she ought to think about it, there was quite a bit of time yet.

The idea had come to me during the conversation with Hartmeier. Of course it would be a challenge to Sonia to bring up the child of my mistress. On the other hand, she was a sensible woman who had her head screwed on properly, and that solution was the best for all of us. We had already gone over the possibility of adopting a few times.

I didn't do anything for the moment. Ivona was in her fourth month, and there was still a chance she would lose the baby, and the whole agitation would have been for nothing. I went on seeing her and sleeping with her, and watched her belly swell. She was even more taciturn than before, and talked neither about her condition nor about any plans for the child after its birth. Only sometimes she would groan and rub her back, which seemed to hurt. Once, when I was getting a glass of water in the kitchen, I saw an ultrasound picture lying on the table, it was a white crooked thing against a black background, but I got no sense of that as my child.

I kept putting off my conversation with Sonia. Finally I resolved to talk to her after the holidays. We spent Christmas with her parents, and then drove into the mountains for a few days by ourselves. Ferdy and Alice had recommended a hotel, a great castle of a place in a remote valley not far from Garmisch. They would come up for a couple of days themselves, we hadn't seen each other in a long time. I had the sense that Sonia was looking forward to it more than I was. We had gone to the office quickly that morning, to sort out a few things, and we left Munich later than we'd planned. On the way Ferdy called me on my cell. I passed it to Sonia, and she talked to him. She laughed once or twice, and then she said, Oh well then, see you tomorrow. They would be coming a day late, she said, Ferdy evidently had even more to do than we did. Fine by me, I said.

We arrived in the early evening, and barely had time to look at our room before we heard the dinner gong. The dining room was full of families with nicely dressed children with good posture, talking quietly to their parents. Sonia had an expression I often saw on her when there were children around, a mixture of rapture and slight sorrow. Her last ovulation had been two weeks ago, I had spotted the red ring around the date on the kitchen calendar, but had gotten home that night later than expected, and Sonia had already been asleep. I wondered whether to wake her, but ended up just letting it go.

From the very beginning I didn't feel at ease in the hotel. Sonia seemed to like it. This was her social sphere, people who were demonstratively hiding their wealth and treated the staff in such a jolly, friendly way that it almost had the effect of condescension. They all seemed to be playing a game, and observing themselves and one another. They were playing at high society, the cultivated art lovers, hurrying out of the dining room to the events hall to catch the chamber music concert, as if there were no other possible way of getting through an evening. Sonia didn't want to miss the concert either, as she said. Please no, I said, I have to go outside for some fresh air, otherwise I'll suffocate. She looked at me in alarm, as if she'd peered briefly into an abyss, but then she gave in right away, and said she had a headache, perhaps it was the altitude, and a walk would do her good.

It was cold outside, there was snow predicted for the night ahead, but the sky was still clear, with many stars and a waning moon. Sonia started to talk about a project we were working on. We're on holiday, I said, forget about work for once, can't you? I had thought long and hard about how to break the news to her, now I just said, listen, I'm having a baby. Sonia reacted amazingly calmly. It must have been that she had so many conflicting feelings that none of them came out on top. She had guessed that I had a lover, that seemed to bother her less than the fact it was Ivona, the Polish girl, as she always referred to her. I was amazed that her first thought was the same as mine.

And that she used the same words I used with Ivona. After all, it's your baby too.

I asked her if it wouldn't be a problem for her. She said her only condition was that she wouldn't have to meet the Polish girl. What if she wants to see the baby? That's up to you. She said she wanted to go home. Right now?, I asked. I can't drive you, I've had too much to drink. I haven't, said Sonia. She didn't want me with her anyway. She needed time to think. You can have your Polish woman come and stay. Her voice sounded cold rather than bitter. Sonia wouldn't be talked out of her plan, and finally I handed her the car keys and helped her with the bags. I asked her to call when she got home.

Two hours later, she called. I had taken a bottle of wine up to the room, and was lying on the bed, watching TV. I hit the mute button when the phone rang. Sonia said she had arrived safely, then she stopped, but I could tell she wanted to talk. It seemed to be easier for her to talk to me on the phone. She said she'd thought things over during the drive.

We talked probably for two hours about our relationship, about our affairs, about our expectations and desires. Sonia cried, and at times I cried too. I had never felt so close to her. We won't tell the child anything, will we?, she said. We'll bring it up as ours. Are you looking forward to it? She stopped for a moment, then she said she wasn't sure. She said she thought she was. You'll make a wonderful mother,

I said. She promised to drive back up in the morning, we
had lots to talk about. Sleep well, I said. I love you.

The next day Sonia was back in the hotel. It had snowed
overnight, and the last bit of the road hadn't been cleared
yet, and she'd been stuck down in the valley, waiting for the
plow to come through. When she finally arrived, we greeted
each other as though we hadn't seen each other for ages.
We went for a walk in the snow, and talked everything over
again. We relished the reconciliation of the night by saying
over and over what we'd done wrong, and how we meant to
do better in the future, and what our life would be like, and
how much we loved each other. Our words were conjura-
tions, as though everything would go the way we wanted so
long as we said it often enough. Aren't we good together?,
said Sonia. Yes, I said, everything will turn out fine. And at
that moment I really believed it. It seemed possible in that
landscape that had transformed itself overnight into a pure
shiny surface.

Ferdy and Alice arrived in the afternoon. Sonia and I
had lain down after lunch, we had neither of us gotten
much sleep the previous night. At about four the phone
rang. It was Ferdy, and we arranged to meet downstairs in
the restaurant in half an hour.

I knew right away that it was a mistake to see those two
up here. He had done the drive in five and a half hours,

Ferdy bragged before we had even shaken hands. He had put on weight and lost a lot of his hair, and even though he talked and laughed the whole time, I couldn't shake the feeling there was something wrong. Alice was even thinner than she'd been seven years ago. There was something careworn about her, and she seemed tired and irritable. She talked a lot too. She was still meeting lots of geniuses and going to astounding concerts and art exhibitions. There was so much more going on in Berlin than Munich, she said, returning to Bavaria always gave her the creeps. I asked her if she was still playing the violin. She wanted to take it up again, she said, once the kids were a little older. They had two girls they'd left with Ferdy's parents on the way here, both, according to Alice, highly intelligent and exceptionally musical. Ferdy and Alice took turns telling stories about the girls, the funny things they said, the searching questions they asked, the profound utterances they made. After a while Alice asked whether we didn't want any ourselves. I didn't know what to say, but Sonia quickly put in that so far we hadn't been able to. How old are you? Thirty-three. In that case you've got a bit of time yet, said Alice. She was pleased, even so, to have had her children so young. Ferdy laid his hand on her shoulder, and leaned right across the table as though to let us into a secret. Those girls, he said, are the best thing that could have happened to us. You can't imagine it when you don't have children yourself, said Alice, but it's an incredible source of richness. Your priorities change, said Ferdy. Some things lose their significance. I wouldn't want to raise children in Berlin, said Sonia.

Alice had a massage appointment. Ferdy asked if we fancied going to the sauna before dinner. I looked at Sonia. She said she didn't, but there was no reason for me not to go. She'd meant to get on with some work anyway.

You're still in pretty good shape, said Ferdy in the changing room, and he smacked his spare tire with his bare hand, I've put on some weight. Alice is a fabulous cook.

We had the sauna all to ourselves. Ferdy asked how business was, and I said we couldn't complain. Berlin is an El Dorado, he said, if you're half-presentable, then you can earn yourself a golden nose. He and his firm specialized in the construction of office buildings, maybe not the most thrilling things to build, but incredibly well paid. His clients thought strictly short-term, he said, buildings needed to be amortized within three years, nobody nowadays planned any further ahead than that. Good design was okay, but the critical factors were being on time and not going over budget.

He talked about the new type of contract where the price was set before the planning began. That way, if you kept costs down, you could make a hefty profit. The magic formula was guaranteed maximum price, and he got up to splash on some more water.

While we rested after the first round, he said Sonia was looking pretty good too. But she was never his cup of tea, too controlled, too cool. What did I think of Alice? I said nothing. She was still great in the sack, said Ferdy. Then he told me about a young woman journalist who had done an interview with him not long ago, and afterward gone for a meal with him. Then over dessert she said, what's the point of sitting around here, why don't you come back to my place and we'll screw. He laughed deafeningly. That's what young women are like these days. He had sat up and was rocking back and forth like a maniac. Everything about him, his way of talking and moving, had something driven about it, restless, that I disliked. After the second go-round in the sauna, I said I'd had enough, and we'd see each other at dinner.

I didn't go upstairs to the room, I went outside. I stood in the darkness in front of the hotel and smoked a cigarillo, and asked myself what the difference was between Ferdy and me. I was driven too, and maybe even more than he was. He had bedded the journalist as if it meant nothing, the two of them had enjoyed a couple of pleasurable hours, and that was it. No hard feelings, as Ferdy said. If anyone had behaved like a son of a bitch, then surely it was me. And yet my relationship with Ivona seemed less contemptible to me than Ferdy's casual fuck. It was as though Ivona's love and anguish did something to ennoble me, and give our relationship a seriousness that Ferdy's infidelity lacked.

Do you ever hear from Rüdiger?, Ferdy asked over dinner. I shook my head, and was pretty dumbfounded when Sonia said yes, she sometimes talked to him on the phone. What's he up to? He's working in a think tank in Switzerland, said Sonia, but she wasn't sure exactly what it was about. Something futurological, the private realm, or evolving forms of cohabitation. That's so typical of him, said Ferdy, anything rather than work.

When I was in bed with Sonia later on, I asked her why she'd never told me she was in touch with Rüdiger. I was the last person who could afford to be jealous, she said. I'm not jealous, I just think it's odd, after all, he's my friend as well. I got the impression you didn't like him, said Sonia. Of course I like him. Things hadn't been easy for Rüdiger. He had fallen in love with a Swiss art student. Maybe you remember her, she was there at the New Year's Eve party. Was that the crazy woman who was working on bread? No idea, said Sonia, I didn't talk to her that night. Elsbeth, I said, that's what her name was.

Rüdiger had met Elsbeth on his tour of South America; he traveled around with her for a while and then brought her back to Munich. She had applied to the Academy of Arts there, but hadn't gotten in, so she'd gone back to

Switzerland. Rüdiger followed her and lived with her in an artists' commune in a farmhouse somewhere in the sticks. Full of people, said Sonia, who don't know what they're about, and who spend half the day high, and call themselves artists, without ever accomplishing anything. I've no idea what Rüdiger saw in the lifestyle. He never got his degree. Instead he'd tried his hand at art as well; along with Elsbeth and the others, he'd run up some socially critical installations in public space somewhere, and scrounged off his parents the whole time.

He wrote to me a couple of times, said Sonia, crazy letters, he seemed to be deliriously happy. I wrote back to warn him, but he took no notice of my alarm, and only repeated how fantastic his life was, and how free and untethered he felt.

Eventually Elsbeth got into harder drugs. Rüdiger gave her money, so as to stop her having to get hold of it in other ways. She promised to quit, then she disappeared for days on end, and when she returned she was stuffed full of dope. There's this park in Zurich where a few thousand addicts live, said Sonia. I nodded, I could remember the pictures in the newspaper. Eventually Rüdiger gave up, said Sonia, I think he accepted that he couldn't help her. He looked for an apartment and found this job in the think tank, but he's still obsessed with her to this day. She keeps turning up on his doorstep, asking for money. I think—I hope—he doesn't give her any. I can't imagine what's so spellbinding about a woman like that, and a life without responsibility and without aims. I thought I could see the attraction myself, but said nothing.

We spent another two days in the mountains. We went for walks and swam and went to the sauna. I gradually adjusted to the setting and didn't feel as nervous as I had at the beginning. Ferdy seemed to calm down a bit as well, and started talking about other things than his money and his success. In time, Sonia and Alice got along better, and on one of our walks Sonia even raised the subject of adoption, though admittedly without going into detail. Can't you have babies then?, asked Alice. Sonia said we didn't know, all the medical tests were fine. With Alice you just take her to bed, and bingo she's pregnant just like that, said Ferdy. It made me wonder if he was really so keen on having kids. Alice had always wanted children, even when she was with me she had gone on about it the whole time. I thought I'd ask him about that, but in the end I didn't. What was he going to say, anyway? In a different context he'd said you could plan a building, but not a life. Sonia had contradicted him, but presumably he was right, and hadn't done too badly with his philosophy.

In the new year, I visited Ivona to talk about the baby. I'd had to promise Sonia to quit Ivona once and for all, and I was grimly determined to do just that. You must understand,

I said, I've been married to Sonia for seven years, I love her. Ivona said nothing, and I was forced to remember how right at the beginning of our affair she once said she loved me. Her presence was disagreeable to me again, but I forced myself to be friendly. Did you think about it?, I asked her. She said Bruno had promised to help her. I'll help you too, I said, whether you keep the baby or not. It's a matter of whether you'll allow our child to be raised free of worry and in a protective environment or not. If you work the hours that you do, you'll hardly have any time to look after it.

By now I had visited the social welfare department, where I was told parental rights were automatically with the mother, but if we drafted a joint agreement, then the child might grow up with us. Even then, however, the mother kept her rights to the child. Adoption would be a more effective method. That way the mother's out of the picture, the social worker said.

I felt bad about taking the child from Ivona, but I was firmly convinced that it was the best for all concerned. I explained the process to her. Ivona didn't say anything. She sat there mutely, staring at her feet. I said she had to decide, and the sooner the better. I wouldn't see her anymore now. She was to call me when she knew what she wanted.

I didn't tell Sonia about Ivona's indecision. I didn't want to alarm her, and I felt sure that Ivona would be cooperative

and everything would go well. Sonia started with her cus-
tomary efficiency to prepare for the child. She found a day
care, and read books on parenting, and got information
from the welfare office about the ins and outs of adoption.
We prepared the little room under the eaves, the one that
Sonia had seen from the very beginning as a nursery. We
bought a cradle and Onesies in neutral colors. I had forgotten to ask Ivona whether the baby was going to be a girl or
a boy, and I didn't want to call her. We bought a dictionary
of names, and agreed on a couple. If it was a boy, he would
be Eric, and if it was a girl, then we would call her Sophie.

When Ivona still hadn't gotten in touch by the end of
February, I called Hartmeier and said I wanted to see him.
I asked him to come to the house, hoping he would be
impressed by our lifestyle. I told Sonia that Hartmeier was
a friend of Ivona's, and he ought to see what arrangements
were being made for the baby.

He came along after dinner. I let him in. Sonia was
standing behind me. She usually went around in pants,
but tonight she was wearing a plain blue dress that made
her look very beautiful and slightly fragile. Hartmeier was
visibly impressed. He seemed nervous, and was uncertain
in his movements and stammered when he spoke. He sat
down, and for a moment no one said anything, as though
we were all waiting for something to happen. I asked Hartmeier if he wanted a drink, and he asked for a glass of
water. Sonia went into the kitchen to get it, and he seemed

relieved, and started talking hurriedly. Ivona had had some premature contractions, and was told to stay in bed. Someone from the parish was visiting her regularly and helping with the chores. I said I'd stopped visiting Ivona, because I didn't want to influence her decision. Sonia came back with a carafe of water and three glasses. Besides, it was probably better for both of us if we stopped seeing each other, I said. It was too difficult for my wife. Sonia filled our glasses and stood behind me. I turned to her, and took her hand. She had put on a tormented smile. Hartmeier, looking earnest, nodded.

Hartmeier stayed for probably two hours. At the beginning, he was negative, but over time he thawed a little, which was probably mainly Sonia's doing. I'd told her we had to settle one or two logistical details. When she realized that nothing had been decided yet, she shot me a horrified glance, but other than that showed no emotion.

I shut the door after Hartmeier, and turned to Sonia to hug her, but she took a step back and looked at me furiously. And what would you have done if she'd said no? I said I was certain we'd get the baby. She hasn't even decided yet, said Sonia. She'll listen to him, I said. I didn't want to alarm you. Then Sonia yelled at me, for the first time in all the years we'd known each other, to stop treating her like an idiot. She calmed down right away. If I had any faith in our

relationship, she said, more calmly now, then I would have
to be honest with her. However difficult. She wasn't a baby,
she could face the truth, but she couldn't stand it if I was
dishonest with her. I gave her my word. Then we opened
a bottle of Prosecco and drank to the positive effect of the
meeting with Hartmeier. He had promised to see what he
could do with Ivona. We had talked a lot about unbroken
families, and then talked about money as well. I had even
shown him the latest set of accounts from the business, and
some photographs of buildings we'd designed. We had spoken about the building trade, and I had suggested I might
listen to a bid from his son on our next project.

And what happens to the child if you separate?, he asked.
I've forgiven Alexander, Sonia said, I'm sure nothing like
that will happen again. I nodded and felt quite convinced
of it myself. Even so I had a sense that Sonia and I were
acting. Hartmeier said we were all sinful creatures, which
made me wonder what sins he might have committed.

We spent the weekend in a mixture of euphoria and ap-
prehension. On Monday Hartmeier called the office and said
Ivona had declared that she was prepared to give the baby
up for adoption. And without insisting on visiting rights?,
I asked. I was able to talk her out of that, he said, to begin
with it will be difficult for her, but in the long run it's better,
especially for the child. From the sound of his voice I could
tell that he had supported me, and even though that was to
my advantage, it still annoyed me. He had allowed himself

to be dazzled by our comfortable middle-class life, and be-
trayed Ivona, the cleaning woman, the illegal immigrant.

That evening we celebrated. We ate out in an expensive restaurant where we normally only ever took clients. I
meant what I said. Sonia looked at me inquiringly. About
being faithful to you. Sonia nodded impatiently, as though
unwilling to hear about it. Ever since we're getting a baby,
I've seen babies everywhere, she said. It feels as though the
whole of Munich is full of mothers and strollers and babies.
That's normal, I said. And by the way, it's a girl.

Only now did we mention it to our parents. We told them
we were adopting a baby, not that it was my baby. Apart
from them, we told no one. Ivona had eight weeks' grace
after the birth to reconsider everything, and we didn't want
to talk to people about it before we were positive we would
get to keep the baby.

Sophie was born on April 17. Shortly before, Hartmeier
had called me and told me how Ivona envisaged the hand-
over taking place. She wanted me to be there at the birth,
and to wash the baby, and give it to her so that she might
hold it. Then she would hand it to me, and me alone, and
after that she didn't want to see it again. She had bought a
pair of Onesies for the baby to wear, and a little chain with a
golden cross on it. I found the whole to-do theatrical if not
slightly mawkish, but I had no idea how to do it any better,

and I agreed. I asked who would pay for the hospital stay, and whether Ivona wouldn't have trouble with immigration as an illegal alien. Hartmeier said there was an amnesty of at least three months following the birth, and after that everything would be reconsidered. As for the matter of costs, it wasn't clear yet, perhaps the welfare department. I said of course I would happily pay for them myself.

On the day of the birth I got a call from the hospital, but it all happened so fast that Sophie was born before I even got there. She had been washed and put away. Ivona lay there in her room. Her greatest worry seemed to be that her plan had been frustrated. The nurse who escorted me into the ward now refused to bring us the baby. It had to get over the birth, she said, and looked at me in rather a hostile way. I said I could always come back later.

That afternoon, I was back in the hospital. The baby was in a little cart with clear plastic sides, next to Ivona's bed. Ivona looked at it in a way I couldn't interpret. I was about to pick it up out of the cart, but she said, no, I had to take the baby from her. She lifted the back of her bed and rang the bell. This time another nurse came, this one very friendly, who, in response to Ivona's request, lifted the baby into her arms. Ivona waited for her to leave, and then she handed Sophie to me without a word.

It felt weird to hold my baby in my arms for the first time. Sophie was incredibly light. Her face was reddened, and looked somehow birdlike. I thought briefly about Ivona's appearance, and of the fact that Sophie had some of her genes too, but then I felt ashamed. Anyway, I thought, all babies are ugly. For the most part, Sophie struck me as a completely independent being from the outset, a creature that might be biologically descended from Ivona and me but that really had very little to do with us. I thought I ought to say something. I'll look after her, I said. I promise.

Sophie started bawling. What's the matter with her?, I asked. Ivona said nothing, maybe she wanted to demonstrate that I was responsible for the baby from now on. I went out into the corridor and looked for a nurse. She picked Sophie up and sniffed her bottom. Your first?, she asked, and when I nodded, she said in that case she'd help me. After we changed Sophie's diapers, the nurse put her in one of the little cribs. I went back to Ivona's room, but she wasn't there. In the office I was told she was just having a checkup, she had said I could take the child. Those were her words, said the head nurse, looking indignant.

A midwife came along and told me a thousand and one things I needed to know, most of which I forgot immediately, and handed me a cardboard box with samples of baby care products and formula.

On the drive home I thought about Ivona. I wondered what feelings she had for Sophie. I was firmly convinced that we had decided on the best solution, but I was afraid Ivona would think I had stolen her baby. I would have liked to talk about it with her, I sort of wanted her blessing, but that was probably asking for too much.

Throughout the drive, Sophie had stayed absolutely silent. When I parked, I saw that she had fallen asleep. I lifted her out of the car in her baby seat and carried her into the house. Sonia must have heard the car pull in, because she opened the door, and after a quick look at the baby, led the way up the stairs to the nursery. Then she stopped, not knowing what to do. I put the baby seat on the ground and squatted down next to it. Look, I said, here's our baby. Sonia came closer and asked whether everything was okay. Couldn't be better, I said. Sonia sat down next to me cross-legged and started to cry. After a while, she asked, what do we do now? I don't know. Wait for her to wake up. For the first time, Sonia looked at the baby closely. She stroked the back of its hand with one finger. Black hair, she said, I always wanted to have black hair when I was little. Like the American Indians. Like Nscho-tschi, I said. No, said Sonia, I wanted to be Winnetou, not the girl. She turned to me and asked what effect Sophie would have on our life together. I don't know. Come on, she said, let's have a cup of coffee first.

We were still sitting over our coffee when Sophie started to yell, and I raced upstairs, as though there wasn't a second to lose. Bring her down, Sonia called after me, she's sure to be hungry. When I came back, she was already preparing a bottle of formula. She tested the temperature with the back of her hand and settled down on the sofa. Give her to me, she said, and opened her blouse and bared her breast. Sophie moved her mouth here and there questingly, until she got Sonia's nipple in it, and started sucking greedily. I looked at Sonia, but she was concentrated entirely on the baby. When it took its head off the breast for a moment, she gave the baby the bottle. Only now did she look at me. She must have caught my puzzled expression. She said she had been to the lactation consultant, and had learned that even adoptive mothers can breast-feed their children. Usually the milk wasn't enough, but it was worth it just the same. And you can do it just like that? I prepared myself, said Sonia. She had massaged her breasts every day for months, without breathing a word of it to me. The notion had something alienating, even off-putting to me. Of course it was idiotic to feel that way, but for a moment I thought Sonia wanted to take my baby away. The next day as well she set Sophie on her breast, until I asked whether she hadn't proved her point. Sonia said it was important for the lactation. I didn't like it when she talked about her body as if it were a machine, but I'd already noticed women tended to do that. I never got used to the sight of Sonia breast-feeding. She seemed to get a kick out of it. When I said something, she would reply, you're just jealous. She didn't give up until Sophie was a year old.

For the time being Sophie stayed in our bedroom. We set the crib right next to our bed, afraid we might not hear her otherwise. When she cried at night, Sonia picked her up automatically and took her out. I rolled over and fell right back to sleep.

The following morning, I paid one more visit to Ivona in the hospital. She didn't say a word, and I didn't say much either. I didn't mention Sophie, only asked her how she was feeling, and when she would be able to go home, and if she had everything she needed. When I offered to support her financially, she shook her head, and turned to the wall. Then Hartmeier came in with a little bunch of flowers, and I left.

A ntje looked at me silently. After a while she said she had thought it couldn't get any worse. Is it so bad then?, I asked. What do you think? Try and put yourself in her shoes. She falls in love with a man who uses her as he pleases, and ends up paying her for it too. She gets pregnant, and hopes they will now start a family together, instead of which he takes her baby away from her, and she's left with nothing. I said I had recently heard a sentence in a film that made sense to me: you are what you love, not who loves you. I need to think about that, said Antje, and she filled up her glass. After a while, she said the sentence sounded very Catholic to her. What did I mean by it? That

Ivona's happiness didn't depend on me. Someone in love is always to be envied, whether his love is fulfilled or not. That's stupid, said Antje. It would mean that an unfulfilled love is just as happy as a fulfilled one. That's not how I meant it, I said, all I meant is that it's worse not to love than not to be loved. It sounds as though you're trying to get off the hook. Just the opposite, I said. My guilt has nothing to do with Ivona, just as her love has nothing to do with me. That's all too theoretical for me, said Antje. The fact remains that you've taken advantage of her. She furrowed her brow and looked skeptical. Somehow I still have the feeling that you haven't played any real part in this whole business. It was you who did the damage, but somehow it's all about Ivona. Ivona and Sonia. And Sophie, I said. I knew about Sophie, said Antje. More or less. Sonia told me about it three years ago during your crisis. She said Sophie was the daughter of your lover, but that's not really a true description.

Basically, everything was perfect, I said, there was nothing I didn't like about Sonia, and my life was exactly the way I wanted it. Then I saw Ivona again, and it was as though she had some power over me. I knew what harm I was doing, and that there was next to no chance that Sonia wouldn't find out. But I had no choice, I couldn't help myself. Antje said I was making things a bit too easy for myself. She believed in free will. Has it never happened to you, I said, that you did something, even though you knew it was wrong? That's a part of free will too. Antje shrugged her shoulders. Maybe if you're a kid or something.

I wondered what sort of image Sonia had of Ivona. She had never seen her, and I never talked about her either. I suppose she assumed Ivona must be superior to her in some respect, voluptuous or passionate or whatever. I had to laugh. Antje asked me what I was thinking about, and I told her. Would you like to meet the man with whom Sonia deceived you?, she asked. There was a fling she had once with an old school friend I vaguely knew, I said, but she was tipsy. For her, that was extenuating circumstances, for me it only made it worse. I wanted to know who it was, until she finally told me. After that, I wished I'd never known. For a while I was completely paranoid. Every time she left the office, I thought she was on her way to him. Antje said as long as Sonia didn't know Ivona, she could pretend she didn't really exist. Ivona's just a name to her. Only if Sonia were to meet her would the name acquire a face, never mind how attractive or otherwise.

Antje asked whether Sophie knew who her mother was. She doesn't even know she's adopted, I said, and if Sonia has her way, she never will either. You'll see, said Antje. But one day you'll have to tell her. I asked her how Sonia was doing. Shouldn't you ask her yourself? If I ask her, it's always the same, she's fine. Antje smiled. That's what you want to hear, isn't it? She asked me if I'd ever really loved Sonia. As if it was easy to say, I said. I had to think of our wedding, and the promises we made to one another, promises I didn't believe in at the time. I shook my head. I don't know. Did you love Ivona then?, asked Antje. I've got to go to bed, I said. If you like, I'll continue tomorrow. I more or less know the rest, said Antje. I met Ivona again. Antje raised her eyebrows. Well, well. She got up and said she'd better get to sleep, there was always tomorrow. Do you need anything?, I asked. Antje shook her head. Good night. I remained seated, I wasn't tired yet. I asked myself whether Antje didn't have a point, whether we'd have to tell Sophie that Sonia wasn't her biological mother. It wouldn't have been any trouble for me, if I'd had the least hope that Ivona had any feelings for the girl. But she seemed not to. Perhaps she'd denied them to herself.

Years passed after Sophie's birth, in which I heard nothing from Ivona. To begin with, I still used to call Hartmeier from time to time and ask after her, but once he said she had stopped going to the Bible group, and he had lost contact with her. She'd become a burden on all of us, he said. The whole business with the baby and her stubborn silence. Ivona hadn't wanted to see what terrible mistakes she had perpetrated, so they had suggested she stop coming. And some seeds, he said, fell among thorns, and the thorns sprung up and choked them.

I had expected Ivona to get in touch on Sophie's birthday, and send a gift or at the very least a card. When we heard nothing from her, I tried to call, but the number was no longer valid, and I made no further attempt to find her. Maybe she's gone back to Poland, I thought, it would be the best thing for all of us.

It had taken us a while to adjust to Sophie. Other parents have nine months in which to get used to the idea of having a baby. Even after Sophie came to us, we still weren't sure we would be able to keep her. Only when we got Ivona's final release form in our hands at the end of eight weeks did we dare to see Sophie as ours, and include her in our plans and thoughts.

Even so, our initial feeling of strangeness was slow to yield. Sometimes I forgot about Sophie, and was surprised, coming home at night, to run into her with the nanny, who was looking after her for the first six months. Sonia often got home later than I did, her new role took even more getting used to than mine did. But however difficult the changes, she never talked about them, and she never let Sophie sense them either. On the contrary, she was very tender to her, and almost overprotective. She was forever putting her to her breast. And whatever Sophie managed to pick up, Sonia saw it as a potential threat, poisonous paints, sharp edges, little objects that she might swallow. Just imagine if something were to happen to her, she said. Nothing will happen to her, I said.

Sometimes I would gaze at Sophie for a long time, and seek similarities to Ivona or to me, and not find any. She's like you, I would say to Sonia, who would laugh and say, she's not like anyone, she's unique. And then I would catch her watching Sophie, and I wondered what was going through her head.

At the end of six months, we left Sophie in day care. When I took her in the very first time, I felt terrible, it was as though I was setting her out in the wilderness. But she seemed happy enough to be together with other children. At night she didn't want to come home, and she started crying when I picked her up and took her in my arms.

Sophie was a quiet, placid child, and little trouble. She had a healthy appetite, and put on weight so quickly that Sonia said she was getting fat, we had to keep an eye on her diet. Even at an early age, Sophie was capable of amusing herself. Sometimes I watched her lying on a blanket on the floor, raptly watching something, or endlessly repeating the same gesture with her hand, reaching for a toy or a stuffed animal nearby. When she was older she looked after her dolls with the devotion of a real mother. She fed them and put them to bed, and told them weird goodnight stories that she'd gotten from God knows where. When I asked her about them, she didn't say anything. She wasn't an unfriendly girl, but she was very wrapped up in herself, and seemed to live in a world of her own. Sometimes I had the impression that nothing of the love I felt for her was reciprocated, as though my feelings vanished into a black hole.

Sophie was slower than the other kids in everything, it was a long time before she was walking, and at the age of two she still didn't speak a word. Birgit, Sonia's gynecologist and Sophie's godmother, said none of that mattered. The main thing was that she was healthy. Sonia seemed disappointed, though she would never have admitted it. She wanted Birgit to conduct some tests, but Birgit refused. Just give her time, she has her own rhythm.

Birgit and Sonia usually arranged their medical appointments at the end of the afternoon, and we would go out together afterward. Once, Birgit said Tania had written to her. She had three children with her Swiss fellow, and was living in a sort of commune with several other families on a remote farmhouse not far from Lake Constance. They strove to be self-sufficient, and the children were homeschooled. It was evident she wanted a reconciliation with her, said Birgit.

The organization had jettisoned its former nationalist views, and was now busy opposing war and the threat of Islam. Tania had written that she couldn't very well fight for peace on earth if there was disharmony in her own backyard, and so she wanted to ask Birgit's forgiveness.

Birgit laughed. It doesn't matter if those people campaign for spelling reform or against animal experiments, they never change. Well, asked Sonia, will you forgive her? There's nothing to forgive, said Birgit. She enclosed a couple of editions of a magazine that her organization puts out.

The things they say seem pretty sensible at first glance. But if you read them more closely, you'll see it's the same blend of authoritarianism, naturopathy, and conspiracy theories. I bet you didn't know that the twin towers in New York were blown up by the American government. If only the world were that simple! Sonia reckoned Birgit should write to Tania, what did she have to lose. But Birgit only shook her head. No, she said, I'm not getting into that. It's wrong to support those mad systems.

I had heard of several cases of women getting pregnant after adopting children, and secretly I hoped we would have a second child. When I mentioned it to Sonia one day, she said she had been fitted with a coil. I was shocked, and said, couldn't we at least have talked about it first? It's not you that has to hump the weight around, said Sonia. Anyway, we've got a child. I said, wouldn't it be nice if Sophie had a little brother or sister, but Sonia said we didn't even have time to look after one properly. She seemed not to understand my consternation. Since Sophie was with us, she struck me as being more distant than before. She was often in a bad mood, critical of me, no longer jokingly as once before, but with a tetchiness I hadn't seen in her before. Family life seemed to bore her. When we went out for a stroll on a Sunday and later sat down at a café, the three of us, there was often an awkward silence.

Then Sophie would get up and start running around the café, until Sonia called her, and said, can't you sit still for a moment? She finished her coffee silently and got up. Is it all right if we go now?

Outside it was getting dark already. Sophie was holding our hands and alternately pulling us along and letting us drag her. Sonia was still irritated. Stop it!, she said, stop that nonsense! Sophie didn't seem to hear. She carried on, then Sonia pulled her hand away and stalked off ahead of us. At home she disappeared into her office and didn't emerge till I called her down to dinner. Then she was in a good mood again, and said she had been able to get something done. You shouldn't be so hard on Sophie, I said. I'm not hard on her, said Sonia, but she knows exactly how to infuriate me.

During supper, Sophie kept squinting across at Sonia. She wrinkled her nose, and her expression had something cunning. After we ate, she played by herself, but she stayed close to Sonia, until Sonia asked her if she wanted to make up.

Sonia's parents came to visit more often. They spoiled Sophie, and brought her expensive presents, but they never passed up a chance to say what a bright child Sonia had been. Sonia's father had read up on adoption, and had turned into an impassioned opponent. He was especially

influenced by the texts of a former priest who had studied to become a psychotherapist. This man insisted that
adoptive parents could never replace birth parents, and
shouldn't even make the attempt. An adopted child had
a right to know about its birth parents, it needed to know
what they could not give him, only in that way was there
any chance for the child to break free of its origins and
build a good relationship with its adoptive parents.

Sonia's father sat on the sofa, feet apart. He looked from
one of us to the other, as though on the brink of saying
something vastly important. Then he stared at me, and said
it would be an improvement if children were fostered, and
adoption given up entirely. I stood and said that was stupid.
Sophie wouldn't have to know she was adopted. Not to tell
an adopted child the truth can have grave consequences,
said Sonia's father. Children usually sensed sooner or later
that there was something amiss. There was the Zurwehme
case, if we remembered that. He was leaning forward now,
and eyeing Sonia. A murderer and rapist.

Dieter Zurwehme had been arrested following a spectac-
ular flight a few years back, his name had been all over the
papers. He was the child of a German woman and a Polish
forced laborer, and given up for adoption immediately after
his birth, Sonia's father explained. At the age of eleven, he
found a letter from his birth mother. Look after my little
sweetheart for me. But his adoptive parents refused to tell
him about his parents. From that moment on, things went

downhill with him. He resisted all efforts to discipline him, and at the age of twelve committed his first assault, on a fifteen-year-old girl. I think you know the rest of the story, said Sonia's father.

I had to laugh. Do you think Sophie's going to grow up to be a serial killer then? What do you think we should do? Put her out? Sonia too thought her father was overdoing it. She got up and stood next to me. Her father remained quite calm, he was now sitting back again. We knew how they loved our little Sophie more than anything in the world, and that they respected our decision. He just thought we should tell her the truth as early as possible, and give her a chance to know her biological parents. Sonia's parents didn't know that Sophie was mine, we had told them it was an anonymous adoption, and that we had no idea who the parents were. She's five, I said.

To give up a child for adoption is an attack on life and nature's way, Sonia's father said, quoting his psychotherapist-priest, having a child adopted is a form of abortion. The child is refused space in its life. The birth parents often felt as though they'd murdered their child, and were therefore at risk of suicide. There were cases where the guilt of the parents was transmitted to the children, who then proceeded to be self-destructive.

I could have slapped him. There are perfectly good reasons for giving up a child for adoption, I said, for instance there are people who aren't as well off as you are. It was the first time I had argued for Ivona. Poverty is no excuse for emotional obtuseness, said Sonia's father. Sophie came wandering in, and he set her on his knee, as though to protect her from us. If anyone is emotionally obtuse here, then it's you in your stupidity, I said, you and your tidy lives. I'd like to see you get by on a thousand marks a month. Sonia's father remained perfectly calm. They hadn't always been so wealthy as they were now. And unlike me, he knew what it was like to be poor, really dirt poor. After the war, they didn't know on any one day what they'd get to eat on the next, and so on and so forth. That doesn't give you the right to condemn other people, I said. He smiled agreeably. That's a side of you I haven't encountered before, the socialist. I said I had to make a few calls, and disappeared into my office in the basement.

Deep down he despises me, I thought, the fact that I hadn't managed to get his daughter pregnant, and pass his genes on to another generation. He was completely different with the children of Sonia's sister Carla than with Sophie, not more loving or doting, perhaps even a tad stricter. But he took them seriously, stimulated and challenged them, expected things from them. With Sophie he was so indulgent, it felt almost hurtful. It's because she's the youngest of his grandchildren, said Sonia. And because she's a girl. Go on then, I said, protect him too.

At least from that day forth, the subject of adoption was taboo in the house.

For all my passionate opposition to Sonia's father, the argument with him had its effect. I was more and more surprised at Ivona's failure to get in touch. She had to know that I would never keep her daughter from her, that I would have no objection if she occasionally—under some pretext, if necessary—spent an afternoon with Sophie. The more I thought about it, the more heartless I found her behavior. When I mentioned Ivona, Sonia never said anything, though we could talk about everything else much better than we could before. Perhaps our relationship was becoming more objective, but our shared responsibility gave it a new quality. Sophie was the most challenging project we had ever taken on together. Even though she was anything but difficult as a child. She had a lot of willpower, but she didn't use it the way other children did, with hysterics and stubbornness. When we told her she had to do what we said, she would just look at us in silence, and the minute we turned away, do whatever she wanted. Basically, we were relieved that she didn't require much in the way of attention, and was happy so long as she was left alone and not bothered overmuch.

School admission was a bit of a problem for her. The kindergarten teacher said Sophie was still emotionally unprepared. Sonia was indignant. A few days later she brought home some forms for a Waldorf school in Schwabing. I wasn't wild about the idea. What little I knew about Rudolf Steiner was suspect, and his notion of architecture struck me as frankly idiotic. Someone had once referred to him as an overenthusiastic village schoolmaster, and that seemed about right to me. The school syllabus didn't convince me either. In geometry they'll be studying Nordic weaving patterns, I said, do you know what they are? Sonia shook her head. I'm sure it's perfectly okay. Eurythmics, I read, parts of speech expressed through movement. I looked at Sonia. It's just the beginning, she said. At least it's a day school, and they give them organic lunches.

We took Sophie to look at the school, and she seemed to like it. An older girl took us on a tour of the buildings, and showed us everything. She wore a T-shirt that read: I CAN DANCE MY NAME. I looked at Sonia and smirked. She motioned to me to keep quiet.

I had read up a little on Rudolf Steiner by now, and asked the headmaster a few critical questions, to which he gave evasive answers. I had the feeling he himself kept a healthy distance from the more abstruse ideas of the master. In the end we decided to send Sophie there on a trial basis.

Work was going well. We specialized in school buildings and social housing, and had plenty to do. Sonia and I were a good team in every respect. The division of labor between us was even more pronounced now, it was years since I had last designed anything. Sometimes I fished out my old papers, projects I had worked on in college, competition entries from the time we started the business. Most of it looked alarmingly banal to me. But in the drawings I still sensed something of my mood in those years, my determination to go new ways. Nothing was sacred to me then, and nothing seemed impossible. For all the limitations of the work, there was a kind of truthfulness in it, a freshness that our current designs no longer had. I could understand architects like Boullée, who eventually turned into draftsmen pure and simple, without ever craving to see one of their designs realized. It was only in the fictive world of plans and sketches that you were free to do everything the way you wanted. I started drawing in the evenings, usually oversize interiors, empty halls with dramatic light effects, sacral buildings, labyrinths, and subterranean complexes. I didn't show Sonia my drawings, she would certainly have thought me mad, and I didn't take them completely seriously either.

I was content. I liked driving out to building sites and talking with planners and craftsmen, and watching our plans taking shape. Sometimes Sonia said she would like bolder employers, but I think broadly speaking she was content too. The constrained means and tightly drawn parameters seemed to stimulate her creativity. I don't think she'd have been any happier as an employee of some star architect. A couple of our interns had made the leap overseas. Heike, a young and very gifted woman from North Germany, went and joined Norman Foster in London after getting her degree. When she came back to see us, she talked about nothing but work. She lived on her own in a tiny place, had no boyfriend and no life outside the office. But while Heike talked, Sonia's eyes began to shine, and she asked lots of questions, and wanted to know everything in exact detail. It sounds like a nun's life to me, I said. Heike laughed. Yes, in a way that was true. You had to have a sense of vocation.

By now we had more than twenty people working for us. We had moved into new premises in a disused factory we had adapted to our needs. At the opening, I gave Sonia the Le Corbusier quote in a frame: EVERYTHING IS DIFFERENT. EVERYTHING IS NEW. EVERYTHING IS BEAUTIFUL. She hung it over her desk and said, everything is the way it's supposed to be.

The crisis hit us later than the other offices. It began gradually. We were still drowning in work, but no new assignments were coming in. At first, it felt like a welcome respite. Sonia said now she would finally get around to thinking and reading and entering competitions again. But the bills and people's salaries needed to be paid. I tried to the best of my ability to keep Sonia burden-free, but even so she saw how things stood in the office. We were forced to let some people go. I asked Sonia to do the firing, they were her employees, and she was more popular than me. The first desks were cleared, part of the office was sublet, and a depressed feeling settled in. For the first time, I became aware of a sort of whispering campaign. My secretary told me what was going on. People thought Sonia and I were paying ourselves too much, and treating ourselves to a luxurious standard of living. Is that what you think? Of course not, she said, I know how hard you work. We called a general meeting and put the figures on the table. After that the whispering died down, but the atmosphere didn't improve.

The situation affected our health. Sonia got a skin rash that tormented her for several weeks, and my back started to bother me again, after years of quiet. I took to drawing late into the night. In the morning I had trouble getting up, and after a day in the office I felt tired and exhausted.

In early June the weather got very hot. I spent the whole day on a site, and the evening in a beer garden with a client. I sat on a trestle bench, and my back hurt. The beer garden was full of young and attractive people in light summer clothes who were probably going on to other restaurants and bars, or the movies or the theater. I hadn't been out anywhere for ages, and I suddenly had the feeling I was missing out on something. I yearned for the simplicities of student life. Instead of sitting with a beautiful woman, I was with the representative of a local education bureau, discussing fire regulations and emergency

exits. I was bored, and drank too much too quickly. By the
time I finally finished with the client, I was drunk. I left
the car in the city and took the subway home. Sonia was
still up, in the living room. She put her book down and
started to talk about a problem Sophie had had with one
of her classmates. I said I was tired, and she complained
that everything was always dumped on her. I was too exhausted to argue. Can we talk about it over the weekend,
I said, and went to bed.

In the middle of the night I awoke with a terrible tooth-
ache. I looked at the alarm clock, it was just past three a.m.
I took a couple of aspirins, sat down in front of the TV in
the living room, and watched a rerun of a talk show that
had people laying into each other in the most primitive
way. I don't remember the subject, just the ugly, contorted
faces, and I thought what a thin veneer civilization is, and
how easily it cracks when pain or hatred or lust take over in
individuals. I switched off the TV in disgust and got a glass
of water from the kitchen. The aspirins had absolutely no
effect, but the cold water soothed the pain at least tempo-
rarily. I sat on the sofa, drinking a sip at a time and waiting
for it to get light outside.

My dentist said I needed a root canal, and he would have to
put in a post and crown. He extracted the root and created a
temporary filling. He would take another look in a month's

time, and see how things were then. He prescribed a stronger analgesic, and the pain went away, but the provisional tooth was a permanent irritant. I kept probing it with my tongue, it felt quite enormous. The thought of having lost a tooth depressed me; however trivial, it felt like a memento mori to me.

On the way in to the office, I called my secretary. There were problems on a building site, the designer of the facade had ordered the wrong beams and was now claiming it was our fault, and the structure was too weak. I was short with her, and told her to call the structural engineer. Couldn't they do anything without me, what was I paying twenty people for, if in the end everything came to me anyway. Fourteen, she said offendedly, and hung up.

My mood didn't improve in the following days. I had a continual, ill-defined sense of being under threat that never left me, even when I drank wine after work to calm down. Sonia was working on a competition entry, she had two days in which to complete the plans, and she stayed in her office, which wasn't unusual for her. But this time I felt abandoned and crushed. Sophie must have felt the lousy atmosphere. She kept asking for her mother, and reacted badly to everything I said. I tried to reason with her, which only made matters worse. I lost my temper, and she started screaming and rolling around on the floor like a little child. I threatened her with all kinds of punishments, but was too feeble to carry any of them out. At times I felt close to striking her. No sooner was she in bed than I felt rotten, and felt ashamed of my failure.

It was about this time that I started thinking about Ivona again. It was a warm day in early summer, Sonia was still in the office, and I had collected Sophie from school, fixed her dinner, and put her to bed. Then I sat down on the little terrace in front of the house, to smoke a cigarillo. The radio forecast rain overnight. The air felt muggy, and the clouds over the mountains had taken on a dark stormy coloration, with occasional flashes of summer lightning. Down on the lakeshore, the storm lights were blinking, even though there was no wind to speak of. Then the first gusts came, a door slammed, and our neighbor came running out of her house to gather up the toys that were scattered over the lawn.

Sophie came out and said she couldn't sleep, she was scared of the storm. I took her inside and put her back to bed. Are you going outside again?, she asked when I said good night. No, I said.

The air in the house was heavy, and it felt very quiet. I watched TV for a little while and then went upstairs to look in on Sophie. She had fallen asleep. She had kicked off the covers and was holding one of her innumerable cuddly toys in her arm. I pulled the blanket back over her and returned to the living room.

I didn't feel tired enough to go to bed, but I was too exhausted to read or draw. I remembered that Sonia had asked about the catalog of an exhibition we'd been to together years before. I looked for it but couldn't find it, probably it was in the office. On the bottom shelf, with the art books, were Sonia's old photo albums. Back at the very beginning of our time she had shown me them all, pictures of her as a child and of various friends and relatives she had lost touch with and never talked about. It was as though part of her history had come to an end when the photographs were mounted. A few more albums had come along since, photos of our wedding and of Sophie's baby years. Of late she had taken few pictures, and they were in a drawer, still in the envelope from the shop that had developed them. I doubted whether we would ever put them in an album, their occasions were too few and too diverse. I looked at the wedding album, and then the one with pictures of our trip to Marseilles, lots of medium-range shots of architecture. There were almost no people in them. I remembered walking through the city with Sonia and standing in front of a building she wanted to photograph, as a form of provocation. Get out of the way, she said laughing, I can take your picture in Munich any time I want to. But she never did. At the back of the album were the pictures I had taken of her while she was asleep. She hadn't mounted those, even though they were the only true mementos of that trip together. I wondered whether I was in love with Sonia back then. But she was so lovely in the photographs, it seemed a silly question to ask.

I looked at my watch. It was ten o'clock. I pulled out the next album. University, it said on the first page. I wasn't sure I had ever seen these particular photographs. There were snaps of parties, excursions, and the graduation party. The pictures weren't taken on a Rolleiflex, they were small formats, some with a flash, which made the faces look flat and the background murky. Most of them were before Sonia and I got together. We had been in different cliques, some of the people were unfamiliar to me, others I knew only by sight. I didn't even recognize the bars where they were taken. In a few of the pictures I saw Sonia and Rüdiger together, dancing or embracing with overdone gestures and cheesy smiles for the camera. Sonia looked very young, there was something calm and cheerful in her features that I barely recognized and didn't think she had in her. I felt a little envious of her, and envious of Rüdiger for her love. My own student years didn't seem so happy to me. I'd had to work to earn money, and in the evenings we had sat around in bars talking about politics and the social responsibility of architecture, instead of having a good time like the others. There was one party though that I remembered. It was our last year at college, just before the exams. The caption was "Spring Awakening"; that was the theme of the party. Underneath were pictures of students in costumes, standing in front of the cameras in various configurations, probably already sensing that they were about to scatter in all different directions. I saw myself standing between

Ferdy and Rüdiger with a surprised expression on my face, and another time with Ferdy and someone else whose name I didn't remember. And there, behind me in the crowd, was Ivona. I knew her right away, even though her face in the picture was very indistinct. I knew her by her posture, her drooping shoulders, and the straggly hair in her eyes. She stood there all alone, it looked as though she had cleared a space for herself in the crowd, or the others had moved away from her. Her pupils were red dots. I had the feeling she was staring at me.

Sophie woke early and came into our bedroom, and wouldn't leave us in peace until I got up. I told Sonia she could sleep in for a while. But don't wake me too late, she said, turning over. Sophie seemed to have forgotten all about her tantrum yesterday. When Mathilda came running in, she picked her up and kissed and petted her. I meant to apologize to her, I had overreacted, I shouldn't have sent her off to bed without any dinner. But as often after we had quarreled, she was so incredibly sweet and affectionate that I said nothing and simply enjoyed the peace. Come on, let's go buy some rolls for breakfast, I said, dress warm.

It was a foggy morning, and so cold that our misty breath disappeared into the fog as if into a bigger cloud of breath. Sophie took my hand, which she didn't do often, and we walked down the hill to the only bakery that was open early on Sundays. On the way home Sophie asked me if I liked fog. Yes, I do, I said, what about you? Me too. She asked me if I wanted to live in Marseilles. Why do you ask? She said Mama had asked her if she could imagine living there. And what did you reply? Sophie shrugged her shoulders. I said Marseilles was a beautiful city, but not to live in. Me neither, said Sophie. You're just copying me. No, she said, we just have the same taste.

When we got home, Sonia had gotten up and was in the kitchen making breakfast. I sat down at the table and watched her cut open the rolls, take ham and cheese out of the fridge, and arrange them on a plate. She boiled some eggs and poured water into the coffee machine. She asked Sophie to set the table and asked me if I wanted some freshly squeezed orange juice. What's the matter with you? You look as though you'd seen a ghost. I said I was still a bit tired, I'd stayed up late the night before, talking to Antje, and hadn't been able to get to sleep after. Sonia too looked as though she hadn't slept well. She turned quickly, and I wondered if she guessed what we'd been talking about. I thought of the question Antje had asked me after the show: whether I'd ever loved Sonia. I asked myself whether Sonia loved me. She had once likened our relationship to a house we were building together, something that wasn't an expression of either one of us, but that came about through our joint wills. There were many rooms in this house, she said, a dining room and a bedroom, a children's room, and a pantry for our common memories. And what about a cellar, I said, but at that she had merely laughed.

Will you look in on Antje?, Sophie asked. Shouldn't we let her sleep?, I asked. But Sophie was sure Antje wanted to have breakfast with us, now that she wasn't on her own. I don't think being alone bothers her, I said. Don't kid yourself about that, said Sonia. No one likes being alone. I went downstairs and knocked on the door of the guest room. Yes?, called Antje, and I went in. She was on the floor, dressed in a sleeveless T-shirt and leggings, doing sit-ups. Her body didn't look like that of an almost sixty-year-old woman. I said breakfast was ready. She reached out her hand and I pulled her upright. I'm coming, she said slightly out of breath, just as soon as I've taken a shower. I asked her if she exercised every morning. I have a young lover, she said, with an ironic smile, I'm sure he expects me to stay in shape. How young? Half my age, she said, and she raised her eyebrows. A young savage. And? Do you love him? Antje laughed. You didn't like that question, did you? I love him when we're together. But I don't miss him when he's not there. It's straightforward and good, the kind of thing I've always wanted. Is that the way he sees it?, I asked. Antje smiled. I think so. He's a different generation.

We don't try and fool each other. Her smile turned slightly wistful. One day I expect he'll have had enough of me, and he'll find himself someone else. I enjoy it as long as it lasts. She thought for a moment, and then she said, we laugh a lot, you know. She put her hands to her hips and pushed her top half forward, and in a sort of reflex I reached out my hand and rubbed her cropped hair. Okay, leave now, she said, otherwise I'll have another jealous wife on my case.

That day the fog seemed not to want to break, and we sat over breakfast for a long time. Sophie was in her room, doing homework. What are your plans?, Sonia asked. I asked if they wanted to be left alone, and Sonia nodded. Old memories. I didn't believe her. She was the last person to be interested in the past. I'll be in the office, I said, and I went downstairs.

The door to the guest room was ajar, and I stopped in the entryway, to listen to the quiet voices of the two women upstairs. Then I went in. Antje's travel bag was wide open on the floor, the handle still with the airline tag on it with the flight number and the code for Munich. Next to it were her leggings and T-shirt, and a tattered paperback of a Simenon thriller, *La chambre bleue*. I reached inside the bag and pushed a few garments to the side. Underneath was a tangle of lacy underwear, a clear plastic duty-free bag, sealed, from the Marseilles airport containing a bottle of

Swedish vodka, and a charger for a cell phone. At the very bottom of the bag was a sketchbook. I took it out and leafed through it. It was empty.

In the guest bathroom was Antje's toiletry bag, overflowing with little bottles and tubes. I read the names of the products, creams and powders, tar shampoo and toothpaste for sensitive teeth and contact lens cleaner, aspirin and antacid tablets.

I went over to the window of the guest room, pulled up the blinds, and looked out into the fog, which was thicker than on previous days. Everything seemed very intensely there to me. I had the feeling that everything was possible for me just then, I could walk out of the house and never come back. It was a feeling at once liberating and frightening.

I put on a coat and went outside. The drive, which I'd swept only yesterday, was once again littered with fallen leaves. I walked down the street, slowly and aimlessly. I remembered the last time I had had this menacing feeling of freedom. It was the morning after the first night with Ivona, when I stood in front of the student hall and the birds were singing so incredibly loudly, and I had the feeling of being terribly grown up and having my life in my own hands. I felt as though I'd spent years going through a tunnel, and had finally come out the other side, and was now standing on a wide plain, able to walk in any direction.

The street stopped in a dead end. There was a big pasture there, with a couple of cows grazing on it, behind some electrified fence. When I stopped in front of the wire, one of the cows raised her head and looked briefly in my direction. She took a step toward me, then seemed to reconsider and went back to grazing. In the distance, I heard the sound of a leaf blower and some church bells striking ten.

I heard steps, and turned around. It was Antje. She came up beside me, looking at the cows. They're not so easy to draw, you know, she said after a while, especially their rear ends. I asked her where Sonia was. Antje didn't answer. You wanted to tell me the rest of your story, she said. Come on then, I said, and I turned around, it's easier to talk while walking. Antje slipped her arm through mine, and we walked down the street in the direction of the city center. I told her about the beginning of the crisis. It was the first time the business wasn't improving. Maybe that was the thing that discouraged me the most. It had been difficult before, but we always had an end in view, which we managed to reach sooner or later. Three years ago, for the first time I had the sense that things could only get worse. Presumably that's when I started thinking about Ivona again. By chance I saw her picture in one of Sonia's photo albums, a photograph of a party, where she was only barely recognizable.

I pulled out my wallet and showed Antje the picture. That was my objective. I had to find Ivona. I don't know what I thought would happen if I did.

It wasn't easy to get hold of Ivona's address. Her name wasn't in the phone book, and at the Polish Consulate I was told that if Ivona wasn't registered, they wouldn't be able to help me. The agency leasing the house where she had lived before had never heard of her, presumably she had been on a sublease then. Finally I called the Polish mission. The woman I spoke to asked me to come by.

The mission was housed in an anonymous-looking office building. I rang the bell, and a pleasant-looking woman of about fifty or so opened the door. I introduced myself, and she told me her name, which I immediately forgot, and led me to her office. Outside there had been bright June

sunshine, but inside the office it was gloomy, even though
the room was high-ceilinged. The woman sat down at her
desk and pointed to a chair that looked as though it had
been salvaged from somewhere. I was in luck, she said, it
was a quiet morning. I asked after her work, and she told
me about the difficulties of Poles in Germany, pathetically
low wages, long hours, and all sorts of abuses. I had no idea
how many Poles were living in the city. Something in the
order of ten thousand, said the woman, no one quite knew.
And presumably there'll be a few more coming now, I said.
We'll have to see, she said. She didn't think joining the EU
would greatly affect the situation. The women who were
working off the books wouldn't register, so as to avoid paying any of their small wages in taxes. Most of them would
probably stay, as illegals.

I had come up with a story ahead of time, but this woman
here seemed well disposed and so understanding that I
thought I would tell her the truth. She listened carefully
while I told her what she needed to know. I'm not proud
of what I've done, I ended. I expected her to say, yes, but it
was best for the child, but she only nodded. It was probably
best for the child, I said. Who knows, she said. At any rate,
I'd like to get in touch with Ivona now, and tell her that Sophie's doing well, and give her the opportunity to see her.
Why now? I was unable to say. I hope it's not just a matter
of relieving your guilt, said the official, and she went over
to a big gray metal filing cabinet, and pulled open a drawer.

What was the surname again? I handed her Sophie's birth certificate.

It took a while, and then she pulled a thin file out of the cabinet and opened it. She was here three years ago. Needed money for an operation. But we have no money, we can only offer advice. We gave her the name of a doctor who treats patients without visas free of charge.

There was an address in the file, she said, but she had no idea if it was still current. Ivona hadn't given a phone number. She seemed to hesitate for a moment, then she wrote the address down on a piece of paper and gave it to me.

That same day I drove out to the address, which was a building in Perlach, not far from Ivona's previous apartment. I found a parking spot from where I could see the entrance. I waited for a while, then called the office and canceled the two appointments I had for the afternoon. The secretary asked me if I was going to be in later. I said I didn't know.

There was hardly anyone on the street. Even though it was a big building, containing fifty or so units, no one came out for a long time, and no one went in. I started getting hotter and hotter in the car, until after half an hour or so I got out and went up to the door. The nameplates beside the buzzers had only foreign-sounding names on them, but I didn't find Ivona's among them.

I waited. After a while an old woman left the building, and I asked her about Ivona. Not stopping to look at me, she shook her head and scuttled off. A while later, a fat young woman pushing a stroller came down the street toward the building. She too seemed never to have heard of Ivona. She thought for a long time with a strained expression, then finally she said there were some Polish people living on the ground floor. She unlocked the door and let me in. I took a peek in the stroller. It was empty. The woman showed me the apartment and remained standing next to me after I'd rung the bell. She wasn't suspicious so much as nosy. When a frail-looking woman of about fifty opened the door, the woman next to me said the gentleman's looking for someone. Does Ivona live here?, I asked. She's at work, replied the woman, with a distinct accent. She was in a kimonolike wrap, even though it was two in the afternoon. Can I come in?, I asked. I'm a friend of hers. I didn't feel like discussing the whole affair in the stairwell. The fat woman stomped away up the stairs. Thank you so much, I called out after her.

The woman in the wrap showed me in and locked the door behind me. She won't be home till the evening, she said, and pushed past me. I was pretty sure she knew who I was. She walked down a narrow, dark hallway, past a half-open door behind which I could hear voices. It took me a moment to realize that the voices were from a television. At the end of the hallway was a kitchen that was clean and tidy. The window was open, and looked out onto the back of the building, where I could hear children and the noise of a lawn mower in the distance. The woman in the wrap slumped onto a chair with a faint groan, then got up right away and asked me if I wanted something to drink. Just a glass of water, I said, please. She filled two glasses at the tap, pulled a stool from under the table for me, and sat down again with another sigh.

She said her name was Eva. She lived here with Ivona and another friend. Ivona was her cousin. She had gotten her the job at the Christian bookstore where I had first met her. We actually met in a beer garden, I contradicted her, fifteen years ago. She was always stubborn, said Eva, and laughed. I asked her what she meant by that. I warned my cousin, she said, men are the same the world over.

Eva was very different from Ivona. I would never have thought they were related. She was petite and blond. She must have been a good-looking woman when she was younger, even now she was quite attractive. She said she had been married to a German man once. The Germans like Polish women, we have more passion and more feeling than German women. We don't try to behave like men.

My cell phone rang. I switched it off without looking at the screen. I asked how Ivona was doing. Not so good, said Eva. The family had somehow gotten wind of her pregnancy, not from her, she swore, and they had—she hesitated, seemed to search for a word—shunned Ivona. I nodded. Ivona was still sending money home, but other than that she had no contact with them anymore. She hadn't been home for eight years. If she didn't have me, said Eva, she wouldn't even know that her father's died.

Healthwise, Ivona wasn't doing particularly well either. She had these growths. She should have had them operated on long ago, but she didn't want to. I said I had given Ivona money for the operation. Eva shrugged her shoulders. Presumably she sent it home to Poland. That seemed to be her only goal in life, to send home as much money as she could. Half her relatives were dependent on Ivona, and yet no one liked her. She works, said Eva, she works like a crazy woman. By day she looks after a bedridden old woman, and in the evening she cleans offices.

For a while no one spoke. Then Eva said Ivona was probably still hoping that I would one day return to her. She looked at me with an inquiring, somewhat skeptical eye, as though to say: you're surely not about to do that. I shook my head. I told her not to be stupid, said Eva, but she doesn't listen to me. You should have told her yourself. I did tell her. Eva spread her hands. There's nothing to be done. If she doesn't want to listen. You can't force a man to love you.

Each time she had talked to her cousin about me, Ivona had said, Alexander is my husband. That was all that could be gotten out of her on the subject. When she tried to introduce Ivona to other men, she said the same thing. I have a husband already.

Come with me, she said, and she took me into the room directly opposite the kitchen. It was even more jam-packed than Ivona's earlier apartment had been. The curtains were drawn, but in spite of that it felt very warm, and everything was bathed in a reddish glow. Eva pulled open the top drawer of a small desk, got out a thick album, and opened it. On the first page, in ornate letters, was written the name "Alexander." My name was underlined and decorated with twisting flowers that looked as though a child had drawn them. Underneath it, attached by Scotch tape, was a lock of hair. I couldn't remember ever having given Ivona any such thing. The following pages were full of photos of me and objects and places that were connected to me and Ivona in some way. I saw the beer garden where we had first met, the sweater Ivona had knitted for me, the back room of the bookstore. Two or three of the pictures I had given her, after she had asked for them, one came from the graduation paper we had put out together at the end of our studies, a few more from architectural journals or newspapers. The articles they had come with had not been clipped, and there was nothing else written in the album either. There was one photograph I could remember well. It was of me and Sonia at the topping-out party for a school we built a few years back. We had brought Sophie along, and she was in the picture with us, though I hadn't wanted it. Ivona had only included the part of the photo with me in it; Sonia and Sophie had been cut away. Other pages had photographs of couples from magazines, advertisements, couples sitting in front of bodies of water at sunset, crossing green meadows hand in hand, or a man and a woman, in pajamas, brushing one another's teeth. On one of the back pages were photos of Tutzing, and our house. I haven't even seen those, said Eva, she must have taken those very recently. Is that your house? I nodded.

We sat in the kitchen, and Eva told me about Ivona's family. Her mother was a schoolteacher, her father a blast engineer. He had spent a lot of time abroad, working on building sites all over the world. I mean to say the Communist world, of course, said Eva, with a smile.

Ivona was an only child. Her parents were in their mid-thirties when she was born. They were both very devout, but they didn't make a display of their beliefs, so as not to hurt their careers. Ivona was all they had, they spoiled and cosseted her. I remember how I used to envy her, said Eva. She had incredible numbers of toys, wonderful dolls that her father brought back from Africa and from the Caucasus. Each time we visited them, there was a fight. No one was allowed to touch Ivona's toys. She threw hysterical fits if you so much as went inside her room. At school, Ivona had trouble. She wasn't a bad pupil, but she was an outsider. So far as Eva knew, she never had any close friends. She was very quiet and stubborn. For a time, they had tried therapy. She had envied Ivona that as well, all the attention. There was always something going on. Often she was sick, she had these vague, chronic conditions that meant she missed school a lot.

Do you know the story of the man who wakes up one morning as a cockroach?, asked Eva. I nodded. That was how she sometimes thought of Ivona, she said, an alien being that had imposed itself on her parents. They did everything for her, but I think somehow she always remained foreign to them. It was as though she had armor plating that no one could get through.

I asked if Ivona had been religious already back then. Not especially, said Eva, she's far too selfish. She hesitated. No, there was a time she said she wanted to become a nun. But presumably that was just another one of her overreactions. She probably thought she'd become a saint, not an ordinary nun.

When other girls of her age started going out with boys, Ivona retreated even more into herself. She was an early developer, by the time she was twelve she already had proper breasts, and Ivona's parents were terrified that she would get involved with somebody. She didn't know what it was they had said to her, said Eva, but whenever a man showed up, Ivona would run away.

Eva looked at me with her clear blue eyes. Presumably she was wondering what I had managed to see in her cousin, why I had gotten involved with her, and she with me.

When she was finished with school, Ivona first did nothing at all. Eva had moved to Warsaw and started a nursing course. She only came back to Posen over the holidays, and then she would see Ivona at family reunions, but they hardly spoke. When Eva had her first proper boyfriend, she practically broke off contact with the family. She was already in Germany when she heard that Ivona was training to be a bookseller. After Ivona had qualified, Eva found her the job in Germany. Ivona's mother had turned to her for help, once her father had lost his job and shortly after fell sick. He had joined the union, Eva said, they were difficult years in Poland. I know, I said, even though I could only dimly remember what had happened. Eva said she had organized everything for Ivona, the job, a room, she collected her at the station and introduced her to other people, Polish girls, and later men as well, good, proper men, who were looking for a partner. Ivona had accepted it all as her due, and never done anything for her. Perhaps they were just too different, perhaps they had nothing to say to each other.

At the time Ivona came to Germany, Eva had still been married. Once she had invited her cousin back to the house. Ivona was so silent that the evening was painful. After that they pretty much stopped seeing each other. Eva would occasionally call the student dorms to ask after Ivona, and sometimes they would manage to see a film together, or go to some event at the Polish mission.

I can remember the day she told me she had a boyfriend. I couldn't believe it. I often asked myself how she met you.

When was that?, I asked. Eva said she no longer knew. I think it was just chance, I said. She must have seen me somewhere, and followed me. Do you believe in that? Love at first sight? Eva shook her head. That was silly, maybe if you were fourteen or something, but not to a grown woman. She read too much, and the wrong books. You were her first boyfriend. I was never her boyfriend, we met once or twice, and then I got married. Then we didn't see each other for years. Eventually she got back in touch, because she needed money for an operation. Eva looked at me inquiringly. I said I couldn't explain what had made me get involved with Ivona. It just happened. It was as though she had some power over me, I said, just her presence. Eva smiled, and said I didn't owe her an apology. Men were like that. She had wondered sometimes whether Ivona really had a boyfriend at all, or whether it wasn't some figment. Ivona had never talked about me, never even mentioned my name.

Only when she got pregnant did I believe her. She called. I asked her if she was together with the father, if they were going to get married. She answered evasively. I mustn't tell anyone. I wonder why she even told me.

Eva visited her cousin in the hospital once, but Ivona gave her to understand she didn't want visitors. Then after the birth she turned up at Eva's, and pretended nothing had happened. When I asked her about the baby she gave me an absolutely terrifying look. Sophie's living with us, I

said, she's fine. Eva nodded. That's what I found out eventually. At first Eva feared the worst. She couldn't say so of
course, but she thought Ivona was capable of anything. As
a child she was once given a cat, said Eva, a sweet little
kitten. She took it everywhere with her. But in time the kitten grew bigger and more independent, and ran off when
Ivona wanted to play with it. Then one day in summer it
was gone. There was a great hue and cry, but the cat never
turned up. Months later, when it was cold again, and we
had to run the heat, one of the tenants found it starved in
the coal cellar. Could it have climbed in through a window
or something, and not gotten out again?, I asked. There was
no window, said Eva. Someone must have shut it in there,
and I'm pretty sure it was Ivona. Even though she made a
great fuss, and had a proper burial for it.

Eva stood and refilled our glasses. Anyway, she said, sitting down again, it's certainly better for your daughter to
grow up with you. Ivona had no time to look after her. I
took out my wallet and showed her the picture of Sophie.
She looked at it briefly.

Ivona had no money, her religious friends dropped her
just like that, as soon as the child was born. She gestured
contemptuously. Well, and then suddenly Eva was worth
knowing again. It hadn't been a particularly good time for
her either, she had just gotten divorced.

Eva had helped Ivona find another job. Later on they'd
moved into this apartment together, to save money, along

with Małgorzata, who worked in the hospital with her. Her relationship with her cousin, though, was no closer than before. On the contrary, since they were living as roommates, Ivona remained even more aloof. Except for the people she worked with, she seemed to have no human contacts.

Małgorzata and I often cook together, but Ivona has almost all her meals alone. She comes home and disappears into her room, or she locks herself in the bathroom for hours. It's been like that for years. Eva tapped her temple with her forefinger, and said, there's something not quite right upstairs. You probably think I dislike her. But that's not it at all. I'm sorry for her, but I can't do anything to help. She's past helping.

Eva had to go to work. I asked her if I could give her a lift somewhere, and she accepted gratefully. While I waited for her to get ready, I looked at my cell to see who had called. It was Sonia.

Nice car, said Eva, as I opened the door for her. I said it was a leased car. My husband had an Audi 100, she said proudly. She said it was probably best if she didn't tell Ivona about my having come by, it would just excite her. I asked if there was anything I could do for Ivona. Just leave her alone, said Eva. What if she needs money for the operation? Eva said it wasn't a matter of money. Ivona didn't want to have the operation, because she wouldn't be able to have children. I did the math. She's forty-six, said Eva, and she's still not grown up. We stopped talking.

Ivona's wasted her life on me, I thought. For the past fif-teen years she's been chasing the specter of an impossible love. You mustn't reproach yourself, said Eva, as though she'd read my mind, it has nothing to do with you. In her own way, Ivona is perfectly happy. She has you. She's been in love these fifteen years. She laughed. Look at me. I had a husband, but does that mean I'm any better off now?

Here we are, she said. I stopped the car, and she got out and leaned down to say good-bye. Can I call you?, I asked. She pulled a little notebook out of her purse, wrote some-thing down, and gave me the piece of paper. That's my cell. I wanted to give her my card, but she shook her head and said, call me if you want to hear how she's doing.

I watched her run up the stairs with quick, youthful steps. At the top, a man held the door open for her. She turned toward him and said something, and I caught a glimpse of a beaming smile.

I sat in the car in front of the hospital, watching people go in and out, hospital workers and patients and visitors. People who might just have heard that they didn't have long to live, and others who had been cured, at least tem-porarily. I had to think of Sophie. A while back she asked me why people existed. I said I didn't know, and then she had replied in her pompous way that people were there to look after animals. Yes, perhaps you're right, I said, why not. That's the answer, said Sophie with her seven-year-old's confidence. I asked myself what Ivona would have said. She had lost everything you could lose, but she knew what she was there for. She had a goal in life, no matter how unreasonable. Perhaps Eva was right, perhaps Ivona was happier than the rest of us.

I called Sonia, but only got her voice mail. In the office I was told she had already left for home. They had been trying to find me, the secretary said, I should phone home urgently.

Sonia picked up. I said I'd missed her call. She interrupted me. We're bankrupt. Come home right away. What about Sophie?, I asked. Birgit's picking her up from school, Sonia said, she'll bring her home later.

I felt almost a sort of relief as I drove home. For years I'd had this premonition that our business was going to fail. I had felt threatened, even though there were really no grounds for it. Now at last the tension burst, and something would change, for better or worse. But by the time I climbed out of the car, my relief was over, and I asked myself worriedly how we were going to get out of this mess.

Lechner, our tax accountant, was sitting at our dining room table in front of piles of paper. Sonia was standing in front of the French window that led out into the garden. When I walked in, she turned and looked at me. Her expression was worried and tense, as though she were thinking very hard. I wanted to sleep with her, there and then. I walked up to her and kissed her on the lips, put my arm around her shoulder, but she twisted away.

The bank has canceled our overdraft, she said, I had no idea it was that bad. I said I hadn't wanted her to get worried. If we'd gotten the job in Halle, we'd have been all right. Sonia asked how long we'd known about it. Lechner stood up, with the last year's accounts in his hand. It had been in the cards for a while. Liquidity was the least of it. Our outgoings were too high, there were too many people on the payroll. Insurance contributions hadn't been paid for the last three months. You'll be lucky if you're not taken to court. What about the firm?, asked Sonia. Does that mean we're finished? If we apply for Chapter Six bankruptcy, Lechner said, then an administrator will come in, and he will decide what happens. Probably all current projects will be halted, and the employees will be let go, and the furniture sold. A liquidation wouldn't realize much, there were just a few desks and computers. Perhaps the administrator would allow the firm to struggle on. That would mean damned hard work for the next three years or so.

Sonia went over to the table and collapsed onto a chair. Distractedly, she picked up a sheaf of papers, looked at them briefly, and dropped them again. I don't understand, she said, I don't understand, how come no one told me anything?

Lechner didn't speak for a moment. Then he said there was another thing too. He paused. As directors, you are personally liable for losses. Sonia groaned. We should have formed a limited liability company, I said. I know, she said, it's my fault. It's not a matter of blame, I said. He would do all in his power to see that we could keep our house, Lechner said. Sooner or later we would have to have an asset sale, but that might not be for another couple of years. We were safe until then. We may as well shoot ourselves right now, said Sonia. Lechner pretended he hadn't heard. The best thing is you try and find a job as quickly as possible. Try and see it as an opportunity. Opportunity?, said Sonia.

After Lechner left, we sat there in silence for a long time. Sonia was on the sofa, drinking her second gin and tonic. I walked back and forth, flicking through the paper on the table, not really knowing what I was doing. Then I sat down on the sofa next to Sonia. She suddenly jumped to her feet. She picked up the telephone, started dialing, and went into the kitchen, shutting the sliding door after her. I heard her say something. It was French, but I didn't know what it meant.

I went out onto the terrace to smoke. A few minutes later, Sonia emerged. She said she'd talked to Albert. He had work for her, nothing wonderful, but better than nothing. I looked at her in bewilderment. Lechner said we should try and find a job, she said. I won't find anything here the way things are. Anyway I don't want to go knocking on the doors of our competitors. How do you think this is going to work?,

I asked. What am I going to do? You finish your project, she said, and then we'll see. What about Sophie? Sonia thought for a moment. It's better that she stay here. It wouldn't be easy for her to switch to a French school. And who's going to look after her? Maybe you could do something too for once, Sonia said crossly, I'm not going away for the fun of it. We're ruined. We've lost our company, and the greater part of our retirement, and the house is being auctioned off. I told her not to exaggerate the situation. You and your wretched optimism, she said bitterly, if you'd started worrying a bit sooner, we wouldn't be insolvent now. You always told me not to bother you with the numbers. Sonia groaned. She had to call her parents and break it to them somehow. That was almost worse than the glee of our competitors. She came up to me, threw her arms around me, and burrowed her head into my chest. Oh, it's all so awful, what are we going to do? I don't know, I said. It's only six months, she said. Albert is building a barracks, and can use some help in the building. I asked her if there'd been anything between them, back then. That was fifteen years ago. Is that your biggest concern? Surely you'll be able to remember if you slept with him or not, I said. No, I did not sleep with him, said Sonia. I wouldn't mind if you had, I said. I did not sleep with him, Sonia repeated. Would you like it in writing?

At about nine, Birgit came, bringing Sophie. They had eaten at McDonald's, a first for Sophie. Sonia always refused to take her there. Birgit smiled provocatively as Sophie gave us her enthusiastic report. Did you have to do that?, Sonia said, but she didn't really care. Now run upstairs and get into your pajamas. Can I get you a drink?, I asked Birgit, after Sophie had gone. One like that, she said, pointing at my beer. And how is it? Is it as bad as it sounded? Worse, said Sonia. Do you want me to give you something to calm you down?, asked Birgit. Sonia shook her head. She said she would put Sophie to bed, and she disappeared up the stairs.

I told Birgit about the situation of the company. She listened and asked one or two precise questions, it was as though she was making a diagnosis. But when I looked at her questioningly, she simply shrugged her shoulders. You'll be fine, I said, people will always get sick. But what if they stop wanting new buildings. They'll start again, said Birgit. Sure they will, I said. The only question is whether we'll still have our company when they do. Well, if you don't, you just start another one. It's only money. Even when we were roommates, I had the feeling you didn't like me, I said. Birgit raised her eyebrows, thought briefly, and said, no, that's true. Why not?, I asked. I think it was because I thought Sonia was too good for you. I suppose I was jealous. The men who hung around her, first Rüdiger, well, he was all right, and then you, and I don't know who else. And then you wanted to share our place with us. As long as it was just us girls, it was all much nicer. Maybe I really wasn't good enough for Sonia, I said. It's not your fault, said Birgit, you're not the only people in trouble. But for me,

Sonia would have had more of a career, I said. She wanted to go abroad and work in a big architecture company. She knew what she was getting with you, said Birgit.

I stood by the window and looked out. There was a thin rim of color in the sky, but the ground was all dark. If there was someone standing outside, I wouldn't be able to see them, I thought, even if they were just a few yards away. I pictured Ivona with her camera, creeping around our house. We didn't have curtains in the windows, it would be terribly easy to snoop on us.

Sonia didn't come down. When Birgit was leaving, I said I would get her, but Birgit said, leave her be, she's probably lying down. I brought her to the door, and we said goodbye. It'll be all right, she said, and gave me a wink. I was shattered, but I knew I wouldn't be able to sleep. I sat in the living room into the small hours, thinking about what had gone wrong and what mistakes I'd made and how I could have averted our insolvency. I thought of breaking up the company, and about having to tell the employees, and that our colleagues would hear about it, and our creditors would come with their reproaches and demands. I had opened a bottle of wine, and the more I drank, the more confused my thoughts became. I was disappointed in Sonia. Of course she was right, there wouldn't be any work in Munich, while I had to stay here, because I had a school building to finish in Lower Bavaria. All the same, I thought her running away was a cowardly thing to do. I would face the consequences,

while she would be far away on the Med, building a barracks with her Albert, and God knows what else besides. I
couldn't imagine getting through all that, and looking after
Sophie at the same time. My thoughts went around and
around, my eyes were almost falling shut with fatigue, but
I was so scared of the day ahead I didn't want to go to bed.

The following months were the worst in my life. The only
way I managed to get through them was by doing what I had
to do one day at a time. Two weeks after our conversation,
Sonia left for Marseilles. The company was put into temporary administration, and every other day the administrator
came along, wanting to know this or that. She had called a
company meeting right at the start, and made it clear to me
that I no longer counted for anything in the firm. She sat
at my desk and rummaged through my papers and began
sacking people, and cutting costs wherever she could. I had
to ask her for every little thing. At least she was trying not
to have to shut the company down entirely. Even so, the
atmosphere was terrible. There were always two or three
employees standing around the coffee machine whispering,
only to fall silent when I went by. I could feel their stares
when my back was turned, and their hostility, as if it was
my fault that the construction industry wasn't doing well.

The administrator tried to cheer me up. In America,
bankruptcy wasn't dishonorable at all, on the contrary it

was proof that you had taken a chance, had had a go at something. This isn't America, I said. She said I should try and hustle for orders, anything that brought in money, even if it was just licking envelopes. I called Ferdy. I hadn't heard from him in ages, and it was embarrassing to approach him for work, but I didn't have any option. He said he was sorry but he couldn't do anything for me, he would be lucky to get through himself. Come and see us, it would be nice to meet your little girl. I asked how Alice was doing, and we talked on a bit in a desultory way, but the old intimacy couldn't be restored, my begging mission came between us, and I felt vaguely despised. Chin up, said Ferdy, with a show of cheerfulness, as we said good-bye.

The administrator canceled the contract on my leased car and got me a new, smaller one, a white Opel Astra. Maybe that was the single worst thing of all. Not that I cared that much about cars, but every time I parked the Astra next to her Mercedes, I felt my failure anew.

As soon as she was gone, I sat down at my desk, even though I felt like an impostor. I couldn't stick it out in the office. Whenever possible, I drove out to the building site in Vilsheim. But there too I noticed how my presence was only disruptive, and a distraction to the workmen. Often I would check into a bar at four in the afternoon and sit through the time until I could collect Sophie from school. We drove home in silence. I made dinner and put her to bed, and then I fiddled around until midnight. I went to sleep for five or six hours, showered, woke Sophie, took her to school, and went to the office, where the administrator was already waiting for me.

The spite of our rivals was bearable. Some were up to their necks in trouble themselves, and avoided direct comment. The whole sector was suffering, everyone was hurting, lots of companies had already let people go. Sonia was right of course, there wouldn't have been anything for her here. She stayed with Antje in Marseilles, and called every other day or so, but the calls were usually brief. She didn't want to hear about the company, and we didn't have much else to talk about. I was pleased each time Sophie took the phone out of my hand to exchange a few words with her mother.

After a month, Sonia came back for a long weekend. It was early August and the weather was beautiful. The world looked lush and peaceful. The green of the trees had already taken on the blackish hue of late summer, and the color of the water in the lake had darkened too. We strolled along the shore, watching the sailboats and looking at the lovely old villas. The kids were playing badminton in the gardens, and from somewhere you could smell the aroma of grilled meat. We read the menus of the lakeside restaurants. Sonia said prices had doubled since the introduction of the euro, we'd be better advised to stay home and eat.

On the way back, Sophie started moaning. Since Sonia's return she had hardly spoken to her, and wouldn't hold her hand on our walk. From the very beginning Sophie had a

closer relationship with me than with Sonia, and the long
separation hadn't improved matters.

The next morning, Sonia was short-tempered and irritable. We drank wine at lunchtime, and in the afternoon,
when she was tired and needed a rest, she scolded Sophie
for not being quieter. She blamed me for things, and she
was cynical when I tried to talk about the future. Even
though she was suntanned, she seemed exhausted, and her
features were harder and thinner, and there was something
unattractive about her. We squabbled all day, and in bed
at night we fell upon each other and made love more pas-
sionately than usual, but the sex had something desperate
about it, as though we were trying to save ourselves. Stop
it, said Sonia, you're hurting me. I dropped off, and we lay
there side by side, sweating and panting. Sonia said I had
changed. I didn't ask what she meant by that. For the first
time in all our years together, I felt ashamed in front of her.

In those months I thought about Ivona a lot. When I
went out onto the terrace late at night to smoke, I imagined her standing in the dark with her camera, watching
me. The notion simultaneously excited and infuriated me.
I imagined hauling her in and interrogating her. She was
obdurately silent, and tried hiding the camera behind her
back. So I stripped her naked, and we slept together on the
sofa, or in Sonia's and my bed. And then, still in the darkness, without her having said a single word to me, I would
send her packing.

Once I called Eva's cell, but I hung up before she could answer. I didn't want to hear any more about Ivona's childhood or her family or her life without me. All that bored me, just as Ivona had always bored me with her saints' lives and schlocky TV movies whose stories she narrated, as if they'd happened to her. When I thought about being with her, it wasn't the yearning you felt for a friend or lover, it was an almost painful desire, something uncontrollable and brutal. On nights like that I sometimes drove into Munich, and sat in the car in front of Ivona's building for an hour, in the crazed expectation that she would sense my presence and come out. Of course she never did, and eventually I'd drive home feeling slightly sobered.

When I came back from one of those excursions, Sophie was awake. I heard her loud crying as soon as I set foot in the house. It was a long time before she would settle down, and I was so exhausted from my exaltation that I ended up yelling at her and threatened to leave again if she didn't cut it out. The whole time I felt as though I was somehow standing outside myself, watching, disgusted by my own heartlessness. But I couldn't help myself, and that only deepened my fury and my self-disgust.

We had deadline issues on the building site. Perhaps I'd been too optimistic in my planning, perhaps it was the builders' fault. At our meetings I would urge them on and threaten

them with breach-of-contract suits. But by now everyone
knew about the moribund state of the business, and when
I swore at them, they avoided eye contact and scribbled on
pieces of paper. July had been rainy, which contributed to
some of the delays. In August the weather improved, and
finally things got going on site. But in the middle of the
month the plumbers' foreman fell from a scaffold and was
badly hurt. When I got to the site, he had already been
taken away. The workers were standing around, talking. No
one could explain to me what happened, everyone had just
heard a cry and then the sound of the impact. The scaffold-
ing was solid, that was checked up on right away. So what
was it?, I asked. They said he had been an approachable
guy. The ambulance men had carried him away on a gur-
ney. That doesn't necessarily mean anything, I said. They
looked daggers at me and went back to work. The next day
we learned that the plumber had broken four vertebrae in
his spine. The spinal cord wasn't affected, but he would
be gone for at least a couple of months. At least it was no
problem finding someone else in the current climate.

I started drinking more heavily. I spent a long time over
lunch, drinking beer and sometimes wine, until I felt tired,
and work was out of the question. I knew it was stupid, but
I thought alcohol helped me relax. After I'd had a few, the
situation didn't seem so hopeless, and my mood brightened
a bit. After hours I continued. Once, when I was driving Sophie home, I missed a set of lights and almost hit another

car. After that I stopped drinking in the daytime, but more than made up for it at night. Soon I couldn't go to sleep without alcohol.

Once in that time Rüdiger called. He wanted to talk to Sonia, and when I told him she wasn't there, he agreed to talk to me. Sonia's in Marseilles, I said. Rüdiger said he was in Munich, if I'd care to have a beer. I didn't really feel like seeing anyone, but I'd long intended to quiz him about Sonia, so I said okay.

We arranged to meet in a beer garden, but when we met, it was so cold outside that we went to a bar around the corner instead. The place was almost deserted, the air stank of stale smoke and chemical cleaner, but Rüdiger seemed not to notice and sat down at the nearest table. He was looking good and seemed relaxed. He had heard about our troubles, and he must have been able to tell from my appearance how badly I was doing, but he didn't let on. He talked about Switzerland, where he felt very settled now, and his institute outside Zurich, high over the lake. A little paradise, he said, and—not that I asked him about it—promptly started talking about his job. He talked about spontaneous networks and people who had a sort of entrepreneurial approach to their lives, and kept asking themselves, okay, what are my strengths, my preferences, my assumptions? What am I making of them all? Where am I going, and how will I get there? That's where the future is, EGO plc. And what if EGO plc goes bust?, I asked. Sure, there are some losers, said Rüdiger. The way things are looking now, we're headed for a new class society, where two-thirds of society will have to work more and more to carry the social burden of the remaining third, which can't find a niche in the new world of work. I said, that doesn't sound too good. I'm not here to judge, beamed Rüdiger.

And apart from that, how are you doing? Are you still with Elsbeth? Rüdiger creased his brow, as if trying to remember. No, he finally said, that's over now. He hadn't heard from her in ages. I remember seeing her once at one of your parties, I said, I thought back then that she was a bit loopy. She was working on some project that involved bread. Rüdiger laughed. Her father was a baker, that's what that was about. For a time she made sculptures out of chewed-up bread that looked like those pastry cutouts we used to make at school. Her tragedy was, she didn't have anything to express. Having a thousand ideas in your head didn't help either.

He shook his head, as though he couldn't quite believe he'd ever been in love with Elsbeth. He hadn't found the ideal woman yet. Maybe you're asking too much, I said. The ideal woman doesn't exist. Either they're too young, he said, or they're divorced with kids. For a time I was with a teacher who had two sweet little girls, but I want my own kids, and she said she didn't want another pregnancy. The joys of bachelor life, eh, I said. *Ach* no, said Rüdiger, I'm fed up having to look and chase all the time. I'd like to be able to sit at home and watch a soccer match on the television and be content.

I'd ordered my fifth pint by now, while Rüdiger was still on his first. I interrupted him in the middle of a sentence, and said I had to go to the restroom. As I washed my hands, I looked in the mirror and thought I still looked pretty good, not like a loser or an alkie, just a bit tired. I'd had bad luck. One day I'd get back on track, I was still young, everything was possible.

Back at the table, we sat and faced each other in silence awhile. The place had filled up, and Rüdiger nodded at the corner where a lone woman was sitting, reading a book. Do you remember how we picked up that Polish girl, he said. She reminds me a bit of her. Say, did you and she ever have a thing together?

I didn't answer. I wondered how to begin. Finally I asked Rüdiger if he believed Sonia loved me. He looked at me in surprise. How do you mean? If she loves me. Sure, said Rüdiger. Why did you and she break up then? Rüdiger laughed, then coughed. Beats me, it's a really long time ago. Which of you wanted to break up then? I think it was me, Rüdiger said slowly. How could you leave such a perfect woman? Now Rüdiger started to look worried. Have you got problems? I don't mean with the company. Did you love her?, I asked him. I like her an awful lot, said Rüdiger, she's absolutely perfect, a wonderful human being. He smiled encouragingly. You'll get through it, don't you worry. The building industry will recover, you'll see.

I was sure he wouldn't say anything more about his relationship with Sonia, either out of loyalty or because he really couldn't remember. I said I had to go. Next time we'll all meet up, yeah?, said Rüdiger.

As we left the bar, Rüdiger tapped me on the shoulder. Look, he whispered. A man was standing by the table of the woman with the book. He was talking insistently to her, and she was smiling shyly. Rüdiger walked past me and held the door open. The next story, he said.

I had brought Sophie to my in-laws just ahead of the meeting with Rüdiger. It was just after ten when I rang their bell. Sonia's mother suggested I should leave Sophie with them overnight. I said I wanted to take her home. Don't you think we should let her sleep? I'll carry her into the car, I said, she can go on sleeping there. Have you been drinking?, asked Sonia's mother. Not much, I said, just a little bit. Sonia's father emerged from the living room, newspaper in hand. He too suggested I should leave Sophie with them overnight. He could drive her to school tomorrow morning. I didn't want any more arguing, so I climbed up the stairs and got Sophie. She was half-asleep as I carried her down the stairs. She was clutching my neck and pressing her head into my shoulder, and I had a sense—I don't know why—of liberating a prisoner.

Sonia's parents were standing at the foot of the stairs, with serious expressions. I hope to God you know what you're doing, said Sonia's father.

The house looked terrible. To save money I'd told the cleaning woman to stop coming, but I had neither the time nor the energy to look after the place myself. Often I didn't have any clean clothes left, or I had to wear my shirts unironed. The freezer was full of frozen meals. Sophie didn't seem to mind the microwaved junk, in fact she liked it, at school the food was terribly healthy, and she hardly ever had meat. In fact she was very well behaved throughout the whole ordeal, playing quietly with her dolls when I had to work and going to bed without making a fuss. When I woke up in the morning, I would often find her lying beside me, and it would take me a long time to wake her up, hardly being able to crawl out of bed myself. Sometimes I went back to sleep, and then she was late for school and I was late for work.

I could feel my body disintegrating. The stress, the alcohol, the smoking, were all taking it out of me. One morning when I was sitting on the toilet, I noticed my bare feet, and I thought I'd never seen them before, they were the feet of an old man, the veins shimmering blue through the pitifully thin skin. This is how it's going to be from now on, I thought, my body will disintegrate, piece by piece will fail.

I felt weak and incapable, and without the strength to pull myself together. Even though the state of the business, objectively, wasn't all that bad anymore. While I had let myself be incapacitated by my self-pity, the young architects who were working for us had hustled for work and managed to land a few minor contracts. Just carry on like this and we'll pull through, said the administrator. She talked about it as though it were her firm, which in a sense I suppose it was. We need to convince the creditors that we'll make it, she said. We'll draw up an insolvency plan, you pay down a mutually agreed portion of the debt, and in three years you'll be in the clear, able to start afresh. I said I wasn't sure I had the energy for that. She said you've got no choice. Where I should have been grateful to her, I hated her for her cheery optimism.

I had sworn to Sophie by all that was sacred never to leave her alone again at home, but one night I did it again. Although it was mid-September already, it had been hot for days, and I felt a weird disquiet, a hard-to-describe excitement. I called Antje, but there was no one home, and Sonia didn't pick up when I called her cell either. I worked and I drank, and every half an hour I tried Marseilles. Finally, at eleven o'clock, Antje answered. She said Sonia was already asleep. Half an hour ago there was no one home, and now she's already asleep? Antje said people in glass houses shouldn't throw stones. I said I didn't know what she was talking about. Then think about it, and call back in the office tomorrow. Good night. She hung up before I could reply.

I was quite sure that Sonia wasn't home, that she had a lover, and that Antje was protecting her. I tried her once again on her cell, but once again I was put straight through to the voice mail.

I stepped outside and lit a cigarillo. It was a warm night, and I thought about my student summers, when we stayed up until morning and only went home when the birds started singing, drunk but clear-headed and full of expectation. The house felt like a prison to me, a stifling cell I was locked up in, while life rampaged outside, and all Munich—my competitors, my creditors, and even the workmen on my building site—celebrated. It would take years for the business to clear its debts, years in which we'd have to tighten our belts, maybe live in some cheap hole somewhere.

More or less instinctively, I got into the car and drove off. Sophie had a sound sleep, and I didn't mean to be gone for long. I had had a fair bit to drink, but I felt in control of the car. There wasn't much traffic on the roads, and I got through easily. Half an hour later, I was parked in front of Ivona's building. Maybe she was still at work, and I could pick her up and take her for a spin, or just bang her on the back seat. Then I'd be able to sleep, at long last sleep quietly. I switched on the radio, listened to music, and smoked. After a bit, I opened the window and turned off the radio, to listen to the city and the sounds of the night. Gradually I sobered up. I had already decided to drive home when the phone rang. It was Sonia. Sounding incandescent with fury, she asked me where I was. In the car, I said. Are you crazy? Who's looking after Sophie? She's asleep, I said. Now that I was speaking, I felt tipsy again. I said I was just on my way home. Sonia said I was a fool. And where were you hanging around?, I asked.

When I got home, the next-door neighbor was in the sitting room. She had a key, and Sonia had called her and asked her to keep an eye on Sophie until I got home. She looked sleepy and didn't have much to say, just that everything was fine. Of course everything's fine, I don't know what's gotten into Sonia. The neighbor said nothing. Well, good night then, I said, thanks. I know you're having a hard time of it, she said, but you need to pull yourself together. Imagine if something had happened. I walked over to the door to usher her out. If you want to talk, she said. No, I said, I don't want to talk. Good night.

The following day Sonia's mother called me in the office and said they would be happy to look after Sophie for a while. Has Sonia talked to you? She hesitated, then said it would surely make things simpler for me now, when I had so much on my mind. I wondered whether Sonia had told her what happened. She sounded perfectly calm and neutral. She has to go to school, I said. My husband can drive her, said Sonia's mother, he's happy to do that for you. I didn't say anything. You can see her whenever you want, she said. It sounded as though she was depriving me of custody. I still didn't say anything. I'm sure it's best for her, she said. I said I had to talk to Sophie about it. Then we'll come by tonight and collect her, she said.

I asked Sophie how she'd like to spend a couple of days with Granny and Grandpa. Your daddy's got lots of work to do, Sonia's mother said, when they came around that evening. She promised her a doll that could make pee-pee. And they would go out on a boat on the lake, and she'd baked a cake, a chocolate cake. You don't have to talk to her as if she's a moron, I said. I promised Sophie I'd look in on her every day. I felt like a traitor.

I imagined everything would be easier without Sophie, but it turned out to be the opposite. I started drinking even more, and started looking clearly ravaged. After work I stopped by my in-laws', played a bit with Sophie, then I drove into the city and back to the office, to work some more. When I couldn't go on, I went to a bar where I could be sure of not meeting anyone I knew. I got into conversation with all kinds of people, listened to the life stories of men I would have crossed the street to avoid only months before. And more and more often I told my own story, and got bits of advice back. Just leave them, urged someone who had deserted his own family many years ago. Since then he'd only done the bare minimum of work, so they couldn't take anything from him. Another man told me he'd been married to a Polish woman too. I'm not married. Then marry her, he said. I said I am married, and he gestured dismissively. Women are all the same. Sometimes women accosted me and wanted me to go home with them. When one wouldn't give up, I said I didn't pay for sex. Then what's this about, she asked, pointing to my wedding ring.

That time in my life has turned into one long night, a night full of mad conversations and loud music and laughter. I talked incessantly, not caring whether anyone was listening. My story was just as interchangeable as the man or woman next to me, we all stared in the same way, clutched our glasses, ordered another round of beer or schnapps. I staggered to the toilet, which was brightly lit. Cool night air came in through the open window, and for a moment I thought I could escape, climb out the window and run away from my life, a sort of film scene. But then I went back into the bar and sat down again. The stool next to me was empty, and I could hardly remember the man who had just sat there, listening to me.

At the end of my pub crawls I often drove to Ivona's house at dead of night and waited, I don't know what for. I felt my life had shriveled to a single moment of expectancy. I was no longer bothered by what had happened and what would happen, I sat there in a sort of trance, staring at Ivona's door and waiting.

One time I fell asleep in the car and only woke up when a couple of kids on their way to school banged on the windows and ran away laughing. I felt ashamed of myself when I imagined Sophie finding me in this state, but not even that could induce me to pull myself together. That day I didn't go to the office. I went home and lay down, and when the secretary called at nine o'clock, I claimed I was sick and went straight back to bed. I woke late in the afternoon with a splitting headache that only got better when I'd drunk a beer. I called my in-laws and said I couldn't come by today, I didn't feel well. Sonia's mother said that didn't matter, she thought it was better anyway if I didn't come every day. Sophie had settled in well with them. From then on I only visited her on weekends.

I knew things couldn't go on this way, that I was destroying my health and my family and my company, but I didn't have the strength of will to do anything about it. My decline felt like a huge relief, coming as it did at the end of years of strain. I imagined a life without ties and obligations. I would find a job somewhere and a small apartment, and live there on my own. At last I would have time, time in which to think and reflect. I felt calmer, often it was as though I was looking at myself from the outside—as though this was a person with whom I had nothing in common. Then everything around me became peaceful and beautiful. Sometimes I felt I was waking up in the middle of the street, I was standing somewhere and looking at a schoolyard or a building site, or some other place, and I didn't know how long I had been standing there like that, and I had to stop and think before it came to me what I was doing and where I was going.

When I stayed late in the office, it was just to delay the onset of drinking. I sat at my desk, playing solitaire on the computer until my hand hurt with the repetitive motions. It was almost eleven when I finally left. That evening there had been an important Bundesliga match, and the bars were full of drunk soccer fans. But what I wanted was boredom, I didn't seek distraction, my time was valuable. I found a small corner pub that didn't have a TV and was practically deserted. I sat down at a table and ordered a beer, and started staring into space. A heavyset man was sitting at the bar, who seemed to be more or less my age, and who kept looking across at me. After some time, he came up to my table, glass in hand, and asked if he could join me. I nodded, and he sat opposite me and started talking right away. He had a faint accent, perhaps he was French and had learned German out of books. His sentences were long and complex, and he used quite a few obsolete words. It wasn't altogether easy to follow his account. A woman had died, it wasn't clear to me what the relationship between them was, but he blamed himself for her death. He seemed to be quite obsessed with the idea of guilt. More than once he asked

me if I thought I was guiltless, but before I could say anything he was off again, till I stopped listening and was only
nodding. I thought about his question. I had treated Ivona
badly, but I couldn't feel guilty because of that. If anyone
had the right to reproach me for something, it was Sonia.
But I didn't exactly feel guilty toward her either. It seemed
to me that everything had just happened to me, and I
was as little to blame for it as Sonia or Ivona. I wasn't a
monster, I was no better and no worse than anyone else.
The whole question of blame seemed absurd to me, but
in spite of that I realized that although I'd never given it
much thought, it had always played a role in my life. It
was as though I'd felt guilty from childhood, but not for
anything specific, anything I could have done differently.
Perhaps it was the aboriginal guilt of humanity. If only
I could get rid of this feeling, I'd be free. This insight in
my drunkenness struck me as a great wisdom, and I really
had a sense of liberation.

It's not that one's a bad person, the Frenchman was saying, but you lose the light. He was still talking about his
guilt, but he could have been talking about mine. He had
treated me to a schnapps, and as soon as we'd emptied our
glasses, the bartender stepped up to our table, I don't know
if he'd been given a sign or what, and refilled them, anyway
I drank far too quickly, and even more than usual. When
I stood to take a leak, my chair fell over behind me, and
the room started to spin before my eyes. The Frenchman

stopped in midsentence, and when I came back continued at exactly the same place. He was talking about the most difficult things with a wild merriment like a madman, or someone with nothing left to lose. The more I drank, the easier I found him to follow. His thoughts seemed to have a compelling logic and beauty. It's too late, he said at last, and sighed deeply. It will always be too late. Just as well. Then he got up and left me at my table, in my darkness. I called the bartender and ordered a beer, but he refused to give me any more. You'd better go home now, he said, I'll call you a cab. If I hadn't been so drunk, I'd probably have gotten into an argument with him, but I just pulled out my wallet and asked what I owed. Nothing, said the bartender, the gentleman's already paid. So I am home free, I thought, and had to laugh. The bartender grabbed my arm to support me, but I shook him off and tottered out the door. I'm free.

I sat in the taxi, and was surprised that it didn't drive off. Only then did I appreciate that the driver was talking to me, he needed to know where to take me. I was tired and felt sick. I looked in my wallet, and saw I was almost out of money. Without thinking about it, I told him Ivona's address.

It wasn't a long drive, or maybe I passed out. Anyway, the driver tapped me on the shoulder, saying we've arrived. He waited for me to go to the door and pretend to fumble for a key. I turned around and saw he'd gotten out and had come after me. He asked if he could help. I said someone was just coming, he'd better go. I asked him where he was from.

Poland, he said. I thought that was funny, and took a step back
and would have fallen over if he hadn't caught me. He asked
me what bell to ring, and I said ground floor, left-hand side.

It was a while before Eva came to the door. She was in her
robe, just like the afternoon I'd first gone round there. For
a moment she looked at me in bafflement through the glass
door, then she appeared to recognize me. She unlocked the
door and asked the taxi driver if I'd paid him. He nodded,
and said something in Polish. Eva chuckled and replied,
and took me under the arm. I can still remember the bang
of the lock falling shut, and then the silence and cool in the
stairwell. I felt sick and had to vomit. Eva kept hold of my
arm, and stroked my back with her other hand. She spoke
to me as to a child. She walked me to the apartment, led
me to the bathroom, and sat me down on the toilet. Then
she brought in a plastic bucket and rag and disappeared. I
was still dizzy, but felt clearer in my head, and finally a little
better. I heard doors and murmured conversation, then Eva
returned to the bathroom and said I could sleep in Ivona's
room. I stood and rinsed my mouth out with cold water. Eva
had stepped up to me from behind and held me in a nurse's
secure grip. I can manage, I said.

The room was dark except for a feeble night-light. Ivona
stood beside the door with lowered head. Eva handed me
over to her, and she took me to the bed and helped me
get undressed and lie down. The whole situation was oddly
ceremonial, almost ritual.

I lay in bed and shut my eyes, but I had terrible pillow-spin, and I opened them again and stared at the ceiling to try to keep myself still. I heard noises and, turning my head, saw Ivona padding around, tidying her room. She pushed things here and there, looked at the results, and moved something else. It was hopeless, the room was so jam-packed with stuff, it was impossible to neaten. Ivona's movements became more desultory. She picked something up, stood still for a moment, then put it back in the same place. What are you doing?, I asked. My voice sounded hoarse. Ivona said nothing. She waited there, with her back to me. Come to bed, I said. She took off her robe, turned out the night-light, and settled down beside me.

I couldn't get to sleep for a long time, and I was sure Ivona wasn't asleep either, even though she lay there very still. I was drifting between dreaming and waking. From above I could see Ivona and me in bed, like on those old medieval tombstones I'd sometimes seen in churches, a man and a woman lying there side by side for hundreds of years, with their hands folded across their chests, eyes open, and smiling serenely. Ivona looked very beautiful. I wanted to put my arm around her, but I couldn't move.

When I woke, I felt right away that Ivona was awake too. She lay there as though she hadn't stirred all night. I was ashamed of what I'd done, but for the first time I didn't feel the impulse to run away. I pressed myself against her heavy body, and buried my face in her breast, like a child in its mother's bosom. She stroked my hair, and so we rested for a long time in bed, neither of us saying anything.

Eventually Ivona got up. She slid gently away from under me, picked her clothes off a chair, and left the room. I drifted off again, and didn't wake till she softly touched me on the shoulder. I went into the bathroom, and she to the kitchen. I looked at my watch. It was seven o'clock.

It was quiet in the apartment. I showered and went into the kitchen, where Ivona had already started the coffee. She put out bread, margarine, sausage, and sliced cheese. There was something shy about her movements, it was as though she didn't finish any of them. I sat down at the table. Ivona sat facing me and got up when the coffee was ready. Milk?, she asked. I think it was her first word since I arrived the night before.

I didn't feel like eating, but Ivona had an astonishing appetite, and prepared herself a few sandwiches as well, which she wrapped in clingwrap and stowed in a plastic bag. I thought we looked like an old couple who know each other so well, no one has to say anything. Ivona said she had to go to work, and I followed her out of the apartment and out of the building. The sky was clear, but it wasn't cold. The bus stop wasn't far. Ivona joined the line. You can go, she said, but I stayed standing next to her. After some minutes I saw the bus turn the corner at the end of the street, and it pulled up in front us. Ivona seemed to be waiting for me to say something, and for a moment I was tempted to hold her back. I said I had to get my car, I'd parked it somewhere yesterday. Before Ivona got on the bus, she kissed me on the lips and hurriedly turned away. She found a window seat, and we looked at each other through the glass. All at once I was pretty sure that Eva was right, and that Ivona's life—poor and arduous and unspectacular as it was—had been happier than mine.

The bus had to stop a moment before it was able to enter the traffic. When it finally drove off, Ivona quickly raised her hand, waved and smiled, and then she was gone.

That afternoon was the meeting with the creditors. Sonia couldn't be there, she had too much to do in Marseilles, and anyway she said it wouldn't make any difference to the outcome. The administrator had worked out a plan. She promised to pay the creditors fifteen percent of what they were owed. If I close down the company, you'll get less than five. There was something infectious about her optimism. Even so, the whole business was pretty humiliating. Whether I was to blame or not, I had cost these people an awful lot of money, and they let me feel their anger. One paper dealer was especially vociferous in his opposition to the plan. It was a relatively small sum in his case, but he got on his high horse and lit into me. I flew into a rage, and was about to reply when the administrator put her hand on my arm and whispered, don't say anything, he just needs to let off steam. Finally there was the vote, and the plan was unanimously adopted.

I called Marseilles from in front of the court building. Sonia had been waiting. Well, she said, how did it go? We can carry on, I said. There was silence for a moment, then Sonia said she had spoken to Albert, she was coming home in December. Are you pleased? Yes, I said, I couldn't have stuck it out much longer. I'm terribly tired.

Sonia came back a week before Christmas. I met her at the airport with a bunch of flowers. We sat down in a café in Arrivals. Do you remember meeting me here the first time?, asked Sonia. I was astonished by how beautiful you were. Sonia looked down. When she raised her eyes again, I saw that they were shining. Are you crying?, I asked. She said she had lit a candle for us in the cathedral in Marseilles. In that hideous cathedral down by the water? Sonia smiled and nodded. She had gone there many times in the last few months, just to sit and think. Are you going to find God in your old age? Come on, said Sonia, we'll collect Sophie.

She laughed when she saw the car. I suppose the years of plenty are over. It's not so bad, I said, it even has air-conditioning. Sonia said she had never liked the color of the Mercedes anyway. We didn't talk much on the drive. I just looked across at Sonia from time to time, and then she would look at me, and smile.

Sonia's parents were waiting for us. In the hallway was the little suitcase with Sophie's things, and beside it a new kid's bike, and two or three bags full of cuddly toys and other stuff that Sonia's parents had bought Sophie in the last few weeks. Sophie was sitting in the living room watching a cartoon. When we went in, she looked up briefly, and then, without a word of greeting to either of us, said she wanted to watch the end of her film. Come on then, said Sonia's father, and took us into his office. He adopted a formal expression, and announced he was going to buy back our house from the receivers. He had spoken to the bank and settled on a price. Carla and Sonia's mother were in agreement. What does that mean?, asked Sonia. That the mortgage is redeemed and the house won't form part of any auction. You can continue to live there. Sooner or later you'll come into my money anyway. He got up and said he was doing it for Sophie. And had we noticed how musical she was, we should definitely let her learn an instrument.

On the way home, Sophie told us that Grandma had promised her a kitten. If it was all right with us. Sonia said that wasn't so easily decided, an animal wasn't a toy, if you had one, you had to be sure to look after it every day. Could Sophie see herself doing that? I know all that, said Sophie with an irritated voice, Felicitas has a cat. And you'll have to clean its litterbox, said Sonia. She looked over to me.

I said I didn't think it was such a good idea. No one was home during the day, and the kitten would be alone. She can always go outside, said Sophie. Let's wait a bit, said Sonia. We'll just go home, and then we'll see. Sophie was offended, and wouldn't speak till we had arrived in Tutzing.

I had cleaned the house and carted the bottles off to be recycled. When we got home, it was as though we were in a strange house. Sonia seemed to feel similarly alien. She walked through all the rooms, opening a blind here and a closet there. I was reminded of cleanser commercials, where the woman comes home unexpectedly from a trip and the man has to clean the house in a jiffy with some miracle product. Then they both walk through the rooms together, and the woman looks around in admiration and kisses the man with a knowing smile—because all that cleanliness is just due to her Mr. Clean. Looks good, said Sonia, and kissed me.

It took Sophie a few days to adjust to us. To begin with she retreated to her room and didn't come when we called her down for mealtimes, and complained about all sorts of things. She kept whining about her cat, and when we put it off, she would burst into tears. We explained the situation to her as well as we could, but she didn't listen, and ran back to her room where she did nothing but brood and sulk. Slowly things got better, we went on little trips, she started to talk about school, where she was very happy. Thus far, we'd always gone to our parents' for the holidays, but this time we canceled all arrangements and stayed at home.

When Sophie was in bed, we talked about the future of the company. We were still doing sums continually, wondering where we could save more, looking at competition guidelines. It's not going to be easy, I said. We'll get there, said Sonia, we've got no choice.

The first year was a struggle. We had to bid for every little order, and work for terms we'd have scoffed at a couple of years back, but we managed to stick to the insolvency plan and make the installments. We entered contests, and by and by a few orders came in, little projects to begin with, a restoration job, a vacation home for friends of Sonia's parents. We were working with a much smaller team, and with part-timers. I felt reminded a little of the early years after our wedding, when we were young and inexperienced, and were doing everything for the very first time. Sonia and I worked more closely together than in the years before the crisis, and our relationship acquired an intimacy it hadn't had in a long while. We would often talk about architecture, questions of principle, and what we hoped to achieve in our own work. Everything seemed to be going well, only sometimes I had the feeling I wasn't good enough for Sonia. She had such lofty ideals and goals that I was bound to disappoint her. She treated me with kid gloves, but at odd moments I caught her looking critically in my direction. When I asked her what she was thinking about, she laughed and shook her head.

We set aside more time for Sophie too. We joined the Parent-Teacher Association of the Waldorf school, Sonia worked for the festival committee and helped organize the twice-yearly festivities, and I drew up a plan for a new central heating system.

I stopped drinking, and for the first time in years I designed buildings again. I was much bolder than before, it was as though I had nothing left to lose. When I looked through a volume of Aldo Rossi's designs again, I saw a sentence of his that seemed appropriate. *Seek to change the world, even if only in little pieces, in order to forget what we may not have.*

None of my designs was executed, but that didn't matter, on the contrary, it kept me from having to make compromises, and allowed me to work freely and follow my own tune. I actually felt like an architect again, and that affected my work on building sites.

Sonia's style changed, she had finally broken free of her mentors and found her own language. It sounds cynical, perhaps, but it seemed that the crisis had opened our eyes to new ways of doing things, whereas in the years of success we had barely evolved at all, and just imitated ourselves.

Sonia wrote articles for architectural journals, and was invited to conferences and finally was given a teaching job at Dessau. Then we won a contest for a social housing project in Linz. We're back in business, said Sonia, when she broke the good news to me.

That evening we celebrated. We left Sophie with her grandparents and went to a good restaurant. Do you think we can expense this?, asked Sonia. In six months our probationary period is over, I said, then we'll be clear of debt and we can do whatever we want. I'm amazed we've managed this fresh start. You know the feeling of not being able to turn around, but having to go on and on in the same direction? And the awful thing about that is it has something tempting about it.

If you give in, you don't have to struggle, said Sonia. Maybe, I said. I just couldn't see any way out. Sonia shook her head. Giving up was always cowardly. Even if you lose in the end, it's still better not to lose without a fight. That's what I love you for, I said, your eternal optimism. Sonia seemed not to detect the irony in my voice. That's not optimism, she said, as though offended by my remark, that's attitude.

nd they lived happily ever after, said Antje. Come on, I said, we'd better get back. Sonia will wonder what's kept us. On the way home, Antje asked me what plans I had. No plans, I said. And the affair with Ivona is finished, for good? It's over, I said. Antje looked at me skeptically. Well, let's hope it's over for her too, she said.

We're back, I called out, and shut the door behind me. It was a little after twelve. Antje said she would go and pack. I went into the living room and noticed right away that there was something wrong. Sonia was standing by the window. When she turned toward me, I saw her eyes were reddened. I asked her if she was hungry, did she want me to make her

something to eat? No reply. What's the matter?, I asked.
Sonia's expression had something desperate about it. She
went to the sofa, and then back to the window again. With
her back to me, she started speaking so softly that I could
hardly make out what she said. I pretended I didn't understand, I wanted not to understand.

What do you mean, you're going to Marseilles? I sat down
on the sofa, and Sonia came beside me, with her head in
her hands. I'm not happy here, she said.

We sat side by side in silence. Once I tried to put my
arm around her, but she was so stiff that I aborted my embrace and pulled my arm back. I thought about ridiculous
things, that we'd have to divide up our property, that the
house belonged to Sonia's parents, what our employees
would say. I thought about it all, but I felt nothing beyond
confusion and a kind of terror that was neither positive
nor negative. Was it Antje's idea? Sonia seemed relieved
to be able to speak at last. She said Antje knew nothing
about this. It was her decision, made long ago. When she
was in Marseilles, she'd realized how many possibilities
she still had in her. Is it to do with Albert? Sonia shook
her head. She had never felt at ease here, it wasn't her
world. But you wanted the house by the lake, I said, you
wanted to live near your parents, I'd much rather have
stayed in the city. Sonia laughed, but it sounded more
like crying. We could have talked about all that sometime.
I had the feeling we were getting along particularly well

recently. That's not what it's about, said Sonia. You don't need me anymore.

Antje came upstairs and said she was packed and ready. Was anyone else hungry besides her? Sonia jumped up and ran to her, and led her out of the room by the arm. After about ten minutes, she came back and sat down beside me again.

We talked, though there was no point. Sonia had given up on our relationship long ago, it was just a matter of getting me to understand her reasons and limiting the damage. The discussion went around and around in circles. I contradicted her, maybe out of cowardice, even though I knew she was right. I was reconciled to the situation, I wasn't discontented. But contentment wasn't what Sonia was after. Maybe things will go wrong, she said, but at least I'll have given it a go.

After some time Antje came back upstairs and said she was hungry, and should she fix some spaghetti for us. When she got no reply, she left and came back with Sophie, who was carrying her cat in her arms and looking apprehensively at us. The two of us are going out for lunch, said Antje with a show of jolly determination. Only when the front door closed did Sonia and I continue talking.

What about Sophie?, I asked. There's always a solution, Sonia said. You must think I'm a selfish bitch. No, I said, I don't at all. She doesn't want to go to Marseilles. Sonia nodded, I know, maybe it's better if she stays with you. She hesitated. We're going to have to tell her I'm not her mother. I looked at her doubtfully. She has a right to know, said Sonia. And what if she wants to meet her mother?, I asked. Well, perhaps it doesn't have to be right away, said Sonia. She said she had felt from the start that what we were doing was wrong. Why didn't you say anything?, I asked. I was afraid to lose you, said Sonia. And now I'm losing you, I said. Sonia shook her head. She said we would stay friends. Not much would change. She hesitated. Then she asked whether I intended to move in with Ivona. I think it was the first time she said the name. No, I said, that's over. I wanted to add that I'd never loved Ivona, that she was never any competition for Sonia, but I wasn't sure if it was true, so I didn't say it. Who knows, said Sonia, smiling, as if she didn't believe me. I asked her when she wanted to leave. She said there was no hurry. We hadn't quarreled, and there was no other man in the picture, and she had to organize everything anyway, an apartment, a job. Are we having Christmas together?, I asked, and with that I suddenly broke down and wept. I didn't know you could do that, said Sonia, and put her arm around me, and held me close. There, there, she said.

I was surprised that Sonia didn't insist on taking Antje to the airport. Maybe she wanted to talk to Sophie while I was away, or she hoped Antje would be able to explain it to me, where she had failed. But Antje stayed off the subject and talked about other things. Only when I brought it up, she unwillingly gave me information. She said she had had no idea that Sonia wanted to leave me. On the contrary, she had the feeling that things with us were going better. That's what I thought too, I said. Maybe she stopped fighting it, said Antje.

I asked her about Sonia's time in Marseilles. No, said Antje, Sonia hadn't gone out much. The evening I couldn't catch her on the phone, she'd gone to the cinema, by herself. If there'd been an affair, she, Antje, would have known. That would make it easier, wouldn't it? That would have been a reason at least. I asked Antje what she would do in my shoes. Let her go. You mean, she might come back to me sometime, when she's ready? Antje said nothing. And what if I agreed to go to Marseilles? It's too late, said Antje.

I had to think of the Frenchman I'd met when I was down in the dumps. He too had kept saying, it's too late. It's too late, he said, just as well. Three years ago Sonia had decided to leave me, three years she had stuck it out with me, she had gotten through the probationary period with me, always knowing she would escape me, that she would start afresh when the worst was over. I racked my memory for clues, I asked myself if there wasn't something that would have told me. But Sonia had remained discreet. She must have been terribly lonely during that whole time.

I dropped Antje outside the departure hall. Do you mind if I don't come in with you?, I asked. She shook her head and picked up her bag off the back seat. I watched her go, striding into the terminal building. I imagined her taking a taxi in Marseilles, and coming home to an empty apartment, how she would look in the fridge, and then go and eat something in a bistro. Back home, she would switch on the TV and open a bottle of wine, or look through her mail from the last few days, maybe she had messages on her answering machine.

I imagined Sonia in a small apartment in Marseilles. She was working late, and got home tired but somehow still buzzing. Then she went out again, and met a man. I imagined the photographer that Antje had brought home with her. He sat next to Sonia in a club, she put her hand on his thigh and shouted something in his ear. The two of them laughed, it seemed to me they were making fun of me. I'm sure you'll find someone else soon, Sonia said, you're not a bad match. But I didn't want to find anyone. The thought of hanging around in bars and restaurants and going on dates with women, and starting over, was pretty repugnant to me.

I thought about Ivona. I hadn't seen her since that last night three years before, the only night we'd really spent together. I'd never called Eva, and she'd never gotten in touch with me either.

Presumably they were still both living in the same apartment. I was free to go there and see them, but what would have been the point? Sometimes I would suddenly think about Ivona, something would remind me of her, a smell, a woman on the street, sometimes I wouldn't even know what the precise trigger was. Then I would get out Sonia's photo album at home and look at the picture where I could just see her in the background, her out-of-focus, fingernail-sized face, the only picture I had of her. Then I would wish to possess her again, as I had never possessed a human being before or since.

I drove to the parking lot and walked across to the check-in building. Since the opening of the new airport, I'd flown from here a couple of times, but for the first time the ugliness of the building struck me, the way it was erected without the least sense of human proportions. The handful of passengers who were around at this hour seemed to disappear in the cavernous spaces. They darted nervously about, like cockroaches intimidated by the light. It was as though the building was its be-all and end-all, there only to celebrate its own size.

I sat down in a café from where you could look across the hall. At the next table were two young women with little children who hopped around on the leather seats and were fed cookies by their mothers. I listened to their conversation. They were obviously regulars here, and seemed to feel at ease in this sterile place that could have been just about anywhere in the world. Maybe they thought nothing would happen to them here.

I went to the spectators' gallery. I had once been there with Sophie, but the airplanes hadn't interested her, and as soon as we got there, she wanted to go home again. The only other people besides me on the terrace were a man with two children, who eyed me suspiciously. Then he turned to his children and said, she's gone now, and one of the children, a boy of ten or so, asked, where did she go? I don't see her. There, said the father, pointing into the air, that's where she is. But there was nothing to be seen where he was pointing except the overcast sky. Come on, he said, and then something else that I didn't hear.

Way below, a couple of men in blue overalls and yellow luminous vests were loading baggage into a plane. I looked at my watch. Antje's plane was leaving in half an hour. Slowly it started getting dark, and the colored lights on the runways began to flicker in the cold air. It smelled of jet fuel. Everything, the smell, the noise, the dimming light, gave me an overpowering wanderlust, a desire to leave and never come back, to begin again somewhere, in Berlin or Austria or Switzerland. It was that mixture of trepidation and liberation that I'd only otherwise known with Ivona, and then only for moments at a time. I wasn't happy exactly, but for the first time in a long while, I felt very light and alert, as though I'd come around after a long period of unconsciousness. I rested my back against the glass and tipped my head back and looked up at the empty sky overhead, that seemed so inexplicably beautiful.